BEYOND THE
VANISHING POINT

BEYOND THE VANISHING POINT

RAY CUMMINGS

WILDSIDE PRESS

BEYOND THE VANISHING POINT

Originally published in the March, 1931 issue
of *Astounding Stories*.

This edition published in 2007 by Wildside Press.
www.wildsidepress.com

BEYOND THE
VANISHING POINT

CHAPTER I

It was shortly after noon of December 31, 1970, when the series of weird and startling events began which took me into the tiny world of an atom of gold, beyond the vanishing point, beyond the range of even the highest-powered electric-microscope. My name is George Randolph. I was, that momentous afternoon, assistant chemist for the Ajax International Dye Company, with main offices in New York City.

It was twelve-twenty when the local exchange call-sorter announced Alan's connection from Quebec.

"Hello, George? Look here, you've got to come up here at once. Chateau Frontenac, Quebec. Will you come?"

I could see his face imaged in the little mirror on my desk; the anxiety, tenseness in his voice, was duplicated in his expression.

"Well —" I began.

"You must, George. Babs and I need you. See here. . . ."

He tried at first to make it sound like an invitation for a New Year's Eve holiday. But I knew it was not that. Alan and Barbara were my best friends. They were twins, eighteen years old. I felt that Alan would always be my best friend; but for Babs, my hopes, longings, went far deeper, though as yet I had never brought myself to the point of telling her so.

"I'd like to come, Alan. But —"

"You've got to George! I can't tell you everything over the public air. But I've seen *him*: He's diabolical. I know it now!"

Him! It could only mean, of all the world, one person!

"He's here!" he went on. "Near here. We saw him today! I didn't want to tell you, but that's why we came. It seemed a long chance, but it's he, I'm positive!"

I was staring at the image of Alan's eyes; there was horror in them. And his voice too. "God, George, it's weird! Weird, I tell you. His looks — he — oh I can't tell you now! Only, come!"

I was busy at the office in spite of the holiday season, but I dropped everything and went. By one o'clock that afternoon I was wheeling my little sport Midge from its cage on the roof of the Metropole building, and went into the air.

It was a cold gray afternoon with the feel of coming snow. I made a good two hundred and fifty miles at first, taking the northbound through-traffic lane which today the meteorological conditions had placed at an altitude of 6,200 feet.

Flying is largely automatic. There was not enough traffic to bother me. The details of leaving the office so hastily had been too engrossing for thought of Alan and Babs. But now, in my little pit at the controls, my mind flung ahead. They had located him. That meant Franz Polter, for whom we had been searching nearly four years. And my memory went back into the past with vivid vision. . . .

*****

The Kents, four years ago, were living on Long Island. Alan and Babs were fourteen at the time, and I was seventeen. Even then Babs was something kind of special to me. I lived in a neighboring house that summer and saw them every day.

To my adolescent mind a thrilling mystery hung upon the Kent family. The mother was dead. Dr. Kent, father of Alan and Babs, maintained a luxurious home, with only a housekeeper and no other servant. Dr. Kent was a retired chemist. He had, in his home, a laboratory in which he was working upon some mysterious problem. His children did not know what it was, nor, of course, did I. And none of us had ever been in the laboratory, except that when occasion offered we stole surreptitious peeps.

I recall Dr. Kent as a kindly, iron-gray haired gentleman. He was stern with the discipline of his children; but he loved them, and was indulgent in many ways. They loved him; and I, an orphan, began looking upon him almost as a father. I was interested in chemistry. He knew it, and did his best to help and encourage me in my studies.

There came an afternoon in the summer of 1966, when arriving at the Kent home, I ran upon a startling scene. The only other member of the household was a young fellow of twenty-five, named Franz Polter. He was a foreigner, born, I understood, in one of the Balkan Protectorates; he was here, employed by Dr. Kent as laboratory assistant.

He had been with the Kents, at this time, two years. Alan and Babs didn't like him, nor did I. He must have been a clever, skillful chemist. No doubt he was. But he was, to us, repulsive. A hunchback, with a short, thick body; dangling arms that suggested a gorilla; barrel chest; a lump set askew on his left shoulder, and his massive head planted down with almost no neck. His face was rugged in feature; a wide mouth, a high-bridged heavy nose; and above the face a great shock of wavy black hair. It was an intelligent face; in itself, not repulsive.

But I think we all three feared Franz Polter. There was always something sinister about him, that had nothing to do with his deformity.

When I came, that afternoon, Babs and Polter were under a tree on the Kent lawn. Babs, at fourteen, with long black braids down her back, bare-legged and short-skirted in a summer sport costume, was standing against the tree with Polter facing her. They were about the same height. To my youthful imaginative mind rose the fleeting picture of a young girl in a forest menaced by a gorilla.

I came upon them suddenly. I heard Polter say:

"But I lof you. And you are almos' a woman. Some day you lof me."

He put out his thick hand and gripped her shoulder. She tried to twist away. She was frightened, but she laughed.

"You — you're crazy!"

He was suddenly holding her in his arms, and she was fighting him. I dashed forward. Babs was always a spunky sort of girl. In spite of her fear now, she kept on struggling, and she shouted:

"You — let me go, you — you hunchback!"

He did let her go; but in a frenzy of rage he hauled back his hand and struck her in the face. I was upon him the next second. I had him down on the lawn, punching him; but though at seventeen I was a reasonably husky lad, the hunchback with his thick, hairy gorilla arms proved much stronger. He heaved me off. The commotion had brought Alan and without waiting to find out what the trouble was, he jumped on Polter. Between us, I think we would have beaten him pretty badly. But the housekeeper summoned Dr. Kent and the fight was over.

Polter left for good within an hour. He did not speak to any of us. But I saw him as he put his luggage into the taxi which Dr. Kent had summoned. I was standing silently near-by with Babs and Alan. The look he flung us as he drove away carried an unmistakable menace — the promise of vengeance. And I think now that in his warped and twisted mind he was telling himself that he would some day make Babs regret that she had repulsed his love.

What happened that night none of us ever knew. Dr. Kent worked late in his laboratory; he was there when Alan and Babs and the housekeeper went to bed. He had written a note to Alan; it was found on his desk in a corner of the laboratory next morning, addressed in care of the family lawyer to be given Alan in the event of his death. It said very little. Described a tiny fragment of gold quartz rock the size of a walnut which would be found under the giant microscope in the laboratory; and told Alan to give it to the American Scientific Society to be guarded and watched very carefully.

This note was found, but Dr. Kent had vanished! There had been a midnight marauder. The laboratory was on the lower floor of the house. Through one of its open windows, so the police said, an intruder had entered. There was evidence of a struggle, but it must have been short, because neither Babs, Alan, the housekeeper, nor any of the neighbors had heard anything. And the fragment of golden quartz was gone!

The police investigation came to nothing. Polter was found in New York. He withstood the police questions. There was nothing except suspicion upon which he could be held, and he was finally released. Immediately thereafter, he disappeared.

Neither Alan, Babs nor I saw Polter again. Dr. Kent had never been heard from to this day, four years later when I flew to join the twins in Quebec. And now Alan told me that Polter was up there! We had never ceased to believe that Dr. Kent was alive, and that Polter was the midnight marauder. As we grew older, we began to search for Polter. It seemed to us, that if we could once get our hands on him, we could drag from him the truth which the police had failed to get.

The call of a traffic director in mid-Vermont brought me

back from these memories. My buzzer was clanging; a peremptory halting signal day-beam came darting up at me from below. It caught me and clung. I shouted down at it.

"What's the matter?" I gave my name and number and all the details in one breath. Above everything I had no wish to be halted now. "What's the matter? I haven't done anything wrong."

"The hell you haven't," the director roared. "Come down to three thousand. That lane's barred."

I dove obediently and his beam followed me. "Once more, like that, young fellow —" But he went busy with somebody else and I didn't hear the end of his threat.

I crossed into Maine in mid-afternoon. It was already twilight. The sky was solid lead and the landscape all up through here was gray-white with snow in the gathering darkness. I passed the City of Jackman, crossing full over it to take no chances of annoying the border officials; and a few miles further, I dropped to the glaring lights of International Inspection Field. The formalities were soon finished. I was ready to take-off when Alan rushed at me.

"George! I thought I could connect here." He gripped me. He was wild-eyed, incoherent. He waved his taxiplane away. "I'm going with you, George. I'm almost out of my mind. I can't — I don't know what's happened to her. She's gone, now —"

"Who's gone? Babs?"

"Yes." He pushed me into my plane and climbed in after me. "Don't talk. Get us up! I'll tell you then. I shouldn't have left."

When we were up in the air, I swung on him. "What are you talking about? Babs gone?"

I could feel myself shuddering with a nameless horror.

"I don't know what I'm talking about, George. I'm about

crazy. The Quebec police think I am, anyway. I've been raising hell with them for an hour. Babs is gone! I can't find her. I don't know where she is."

He finally calmed down enough to tell me what happened. Shortly after his radiophone to me in New York, he had missed Babs. They had had lunch in the huge hotel and then walked on the Dufferin Terrace — the famous promenade outside looking down over the Lower City, the great sweep of the St. Lawrence River and the gray-white distant Laurentian mountains.

"I was to meet her inside. I went in ahead of her. But she didn't come. I went back to the Terrace but she was gone. She wasn't in our rooms. Nor the library, the lobby — anywhere."

But it was afternoon, in the public place of a civilized city. In the daylight of the Dufferin Terrace, beside the long ice toboggan slide, under the gaze of skaters on the ice-rink and several hundred holiday merrymakers, a young girl could hardly be murdered, or kidnapped, without attracting attention! The Quebec police thought the young American unduly excited about his sister, who was missing only an hour. They would do what they could, if by dark she had not rejoined him. They suggested that doubtless the young lady had gone shopping.

"Maybe she did," I agreed. But in my heart, I felt differently. "She'll be waiting for us in the Hotel when we get there, Alan."

"But I'm telling you we saw Polter this morning. He lives here — not thirty miles from Quebec. We saw him on the Terrace after breakfast. Recognized him immediately of course."

"Did he see you?"

"I don't know. He was lost in the crowd in a minute. But I asked a young French fellow if he knew him. He did know him, as Frank Rascor. That must be the name he wears now.

He's a famous man up here — well known, immensely rich. I didn't know if he saw us or not. What a fool I was to leave Babs alone, even for a minute."

We were speeding over a white-clad valley with a little frozen river winding down its middle. Night had almost come. The leaden sky was low above us. It began snowing. The lights of the small villages along the river were barely visible.

"Can you land us, Alan?"

"Yes, surely. At the Municipal Field just beyond the Citadel. We can get to the Hotel in five minutes."

*****

It was a flight of only half an hour. During it, Alan told me about Polter. The hunchback, known now as Frank Rascor, owned a mine in the Laurentians, some thirty miles from Quebec City — a fabulously productive mine of gold. It was an anomaly that gold should be produced in this region. No vein of gold-bearing rock had been found, except the one on Polter's property. Alan had seen a newspaper account of the strangeness of it; and on a hunch had come to Quebec, being intrigued by the description of the mine owner. He had seen Frank Rascor on the Dufferin Terrace, and recognized him as Polter.

Again my thoughts went back into the past. Had Polter stolen that missing fragment of golden quartz the size of a walnut which had been beneath Dr. Kent's microscope? We always thought so. Dr. Kent had some secret, some great problem upon which he was working. Polter, his assistant, had evidently known, or partially known, its details. And now, four years later, Polter was immensely rich, with a "gold mine" in mountains where there was no other evidence of gold!

I seemed to see some connection. Alan, I knew, was groping with a dim idea, so strange he hardly dared voice it.

"I tell you, it's weird, George. The sight of him. Polter — heavens, one couldn't mistake that build — and his face, his features, just the same as when we knew him."

"Then what's so weird?" I demanded.

"His age." There was a queer solemn hush in Alan's voice. "George, when we knew Polter, he was about twenty-five, wasn't he? Well, that was four years ago. But he isn't twenty-nine now. I swear it is the same man, but he isn't around thirty. Don't ask me what I'm talking about. I don't know. But he isn't thirty. He's nearer fifty! Unnatural! Weird! I felt it, and so did Babs, just that brief look we had of him."

I didn't answer. My attention was on managing the plane. The lights of Levis were under us. Beyond the City cliffs, the St. Lawrence lay in its deep valley; the Quebec lights, the light-dotted ramparts with the Terrace and the great fortresslike Hotel showed across the river.

"Better take the stick, Alan. I don't know where the field is. And don't you worry about Babs. She'll be back by now."

*****

But she was not. We went to the two connecting rooms in the tower of the Hotel which Alan and Babs had engaged. We inquired with half a dozen phone calls. No one had seen or heard from her. The Quebec police were sending a man up to talk with Alan.

"Well, we won't be here," Alan called to me. He was standing by the window in Babs' room; he was trembling too much to use the phone. I hung up the receiver and went though the connecting door to join him.

Babs' room! It sent a pang through me. A few of her garments were lying around. A negligee was laid out on the large bed. A velvet boudoir doll — she had always loved them — stood on the dresser. Upon this Hotel room, in one day, she had impressed her personality. Her perfume was in the air. And now she was gone.

"We won't be here," Alan was repeating. He gripped me at the window. "Look." In his hand was an ugly-looking, smokeless, soundless automatic of the Essen type. "And I've got another one for you. Brought them with me."

His face was white and drawn, but his hands had steadied. The tremble was gone out of his voice.

"I'm going after him, George! Now! Understand that? Now? His place is only thirty miles from here, out there in the mountains. You can see it in the daylight — a wall around his property and a stone castle which he built in the middle of it. A gold mine? Hell!"

There was nothing to be seen now out of the window but the snow-filled darkness, the blurred lights of Lower Quebec and the line of dock lights five hundred feet below us.

"Will you fly me, George?"

"Of course."

I was the one trembling now; the cool feel of the automatic which Alan thrust into my hand seemed suddenly to crystallize Babs' peril. I was here in her room, with the scent of her perfume around me, and this deadly weapon was needed! But the trembling was gone in a moment.

"Yes, of course, Alan. No use talking to the police. I gave them all the information — a description of her, what you said she was wearing. No sense dragging Polter's name into it, with nothing tangible to go on. The police won't ransack the castle of a rich man just because you can't find your sister. Come on. You can tell me what this place is like as we go."

*****

Bundled in our flying suits, we hurried from the Hotel, climbed the Citadel slope and in ten minutes were in the air. The wind sucked at us. The snow now was falling with thick, huge flakes. Directed by Alan, I headed out over this ice-filled St. Lawrence, past the frozen Ile d'Orleans, toward Polter's mysterious mountain castle.

Suddenly Alan burst out, "I know what father's secret was! I can piece it together now, from little things that were meaningless when I was a kid. He invented the electro-microscope. You know that. The infinitely small fascinated him. I remember he once said that if we could see far enough down into smallness, we would come upon human life!"

Alan's low, tense voice was more vehement than I had ever heard it before. "It's clear to me now, George. That little fragment of golden quartz which he wanted me to be so careful of contained a world with human inhabitants! Father knew it, or suspected it. And I think the chemical problem on which he was working aimed for some drug. I know it was a drug they were compounding, Polter said so once, a radioac-tive drug; I remember listening at the door. A drug, George, capable of making a human being infinitely small!"

I did not answer when momentarily Alan paused. So strange a thing. My mind whirled with it; struggled to encom-pass it. And like the meaningless individual pieces of a puzzle, dropping so easily into place when the key piece is fitted, I saw Polter stealing that fragment of gold; abducting Dr. Kent — perhaps because Polter himself was not fully ac-quainted with the secret. And now, Polter up here with a fab-ulously rich "gold mine." And Babs, abducted by him, to be taken — where?

It set me shuddering.

"That's what it was," Alan reiterated. "And Polter, here now with what he calls a 'mine.' It isn't a mine, it's a labora-tory! He's got father too, hidden God knows where! And now Babs. We've got to get them, George! The police can't help us! It's just you and me, to fight this thing. And it's diabolical!"

CHAPTER II

We soared over the divided channel of the St. Lawrence, between Orleans and the mainland. Montmorency Falls in a moment showed dimly white through the murk to our left, a great hanging veil of ice higher than Niagara. Further ahead, the lights of the little village of St. Anne de Beaupré were visible with the gray-black towering hills behind them.

"Swing left, George. Over the mainland. That's St. Anne. We pass this side of it. Put the mufflers on. This damn thing roars like a tower siren."

I cut in the muffler and switched off our wing-lights. It was illegal but we were past all thought of that. We were both desperate; the slow prudent process of acting within the law had nothing to do with this affair. We both knew it.

Our little plane was dark, and amid the sounds of this night blizzard our muffled engine couldn't be heard.

Alan touched me. "There are his lights; see them?"

We had passed St. Anne. The hills lay ahead — a wild mountainous country stretching northward to the foot of Hudson Bay. The blizzard was roaring out of the North and we were heading into it. I saw, on what seemed like a dome-shaped hill perhaps a thousand feet above the river level, a small cluster of lights which marked Polter's property.

"Fly over it once, George," Alan said. "Low — we can

chance it. And find a place to land near the walls."

We presently had it under us. I held the plane at five hundred feet, and cut our speed to the minimum of twenty miles an hour facing the gale, though it was sixty or seventy when we turned. There were a score or two of hooded ground lights. But there was little reflection aloft, and in the murk of the snowfall I felt we could escape notice.

We crossed, turned and went back in an arc following Polter's curved outer wall. We had a good view of it. A weird enough looking place, here on its lonely hilltop. No wonder the wealthy "Frank Rascor" had attained local prominence!

The whole property was irregularly circular, perhaps a mile in diameter covering the almost flat dome of the hilltop. Around it, completely enclosing it, Polter had built a stone and brick wall. A miniature of the Great Wall in China! We could see that it was fully thirty feet high with what evidently were naked high-voltage wires protecting its top. There were half a dozen little gates, securely barred, with doubtless a guard at each of them.

Within the walls there were several buildings: a few small stone houses suggesting workmen's dwellings; an oblong stone structure with smoke funnels which looked like a smelter; a huge domelike spread of translucent glass over what might have been the top of a mineshaft. It looked more like the dome of an observatory — an inverted bowl fully a hundred feet wide and equally as high, set upon the ground. What did it cover?

And there was Polter's residence — a castlelike brick and stone building with a tower not unlike a miniature of the Chateau Frontenac. We saw a stone corridor on the ground connecting the lower floor of the castle with the dome, which lay about a hundred feet to one side.

Could we chance landing inside the wall? There was a

dark, level expanse of snow where we could have done it, but our descending plane doubtless would have been discovered. But the mile-wide inner area was dark in many places. Spots of light were at the little wall-gates. There was a glow all along the top of the wall. Lights were on in Polter's house; they slanted out in yellow shafts to the nearby white ground. But for the rest, the whole place was dark, save a dim glow from under the dome.

I shook my head at Alan's suggestion that we land inside the walls. We had circled back and were a mile or so off toward the river. "The trees — and you saw guards down there. But that low stretch outside the gate on this side. . . ."

A plan was coming to me. Heaven knows it was desperate enough, but we had no alternative. We would land and accost one of the gate guards. Force our way in. Once inside the wall, on foot in the darkness of this blizzard, we could hide; slip up to that dome. Beyond that my imagination could not go.

We landed in the snow a quarter of a mile from one of the gates. We left the plane and plunged into the darkness.

It was a steady upward slope. A packed snowfield was underfoot, firm enough to hold our weight, with a foot or so of loose, soft snow on its top. The falling flakes whirled around us. The darkness was solid. Our helmeted leather-furred flying suits were soon shapeless with a gathering white shroud. We carried our Essens in our gloved hands. The night was cold, around zero I imagine, though with that biting wind it felt far colder.

From the gloom a tiny spot of light loomed up.

"There it is, Alan. Easy now! Let me go first." The wind tore away my words. We could see the narrow rectangle of bars at the gate, with a glow of light behind them.

"Hide your gun, Alan." I gripped him. "Do you hear me?"
"Yes."

"Let me go first. I'll do the talking. When he opens the gate, let me handle him. You — if there are two of them — you take the other."

We emerged from the darkness, into the glow of light by the gate. I had the horrible feeling that a shot would greet us. A challenge came, at first in French and then in English.

"Stop! What do you want?"

"To see Mr. Rascor."

We were up to the bars now, shapeless hooded bundles of snow and frost. A man stood in the doorway of a lighted little cubby behind the bars. A black muzzle in his hand was leveled at us.

"He sees no one. Who are you?"

Alan was pressing at me from behind. I shoved him back, and took a step forward. I touched the bars.

"My name is Fred Davis. Newspaperman from Montreal I must see Mr. Rascor."

"You cannot. You may send in your call. The mouthpiece is there — out there to the left. Bare your face; he talks to no one without the face image."

The guard had drawn back into his cubby; there was only his extended hand and the muzzle of his weapon left visible.

I took a step forward. "I don't want to talk by phone. Won't you open the gate? It's cold out here. We have important business. We'll wait with you."

Abruptly the gate lattice slid aside. Beyond the cubby doorway was the open darkness within the wall. A scuffed path leading inward from the gate showed for a few feet.

I walked over the threshold, with Alan crowding me. The Essen in my coat pocket was leveled. But from the cubby doorway, I saw that the guard was gone! Then I saw him crouching behind a metal shield. His voice rang out.

"Stand!"

A light struck my face — a thin beam from a television sender beside me. It all happened in an instant, so quickly Alan and I had barely time to make a move. I realized my image was now doubtless being presented to Polter. He would recognize me!

I ducked my head, yelling, "Don't do that!"

It was too late! The guard had received a signal. I heard its buzz.

From the shield a tiny jet of fluid leapt at me. It struck my hood. There was a heavy sickening-sweet smell. It seemed like chloroform. I felt my senses going. The cubby room was turning dark, was roaring.

I think I fired at the shield. And Alan leapt aside. I heard the faint hiss of his Essen, and his choked, horrified voice:

"George, run! Don't fall!"

I crumpled; slid into blackness. And it seemed, as I went down, that Alan's inert body was falling on top of me. . . .

*****

I recovered after a nameless interval, a phantasmagoria of wild, drugged dreams. My senses came slowly. At first, there were dim muffled voices and the tread of footsteps. Then I knew that I was lying on the ground, and that I was indoors. It was warm. My overcoat was off. Then I realized that I was bound and gagged.

I opened my eyes. Alan was lying inert beside me, roped and with a black gag around his face and in his mouth. We were in a huge dim open space. Presently, as my vision cleared, I saw that the dome was overhead. This was a circular, hundred-foot-wide room. It was dimly lighted. The figures of men were moving about, their great misshapen shadows shifting with them. Twenty feet from me there was a pile of golden rock — chunks of gold the size of a man's fist, or his head, and larger, heaped loosely into a mound ten feet high.

Beyond this pile of ore, near the center of the room, twenty feet above the concrete floor, there was a large hanging electrolier. It cast a circular glow downward. Under it I saw a low platform raised a foot or two above the ground. A giant electro-microscope was hung with its twenty foot cylinder above the platform. Its intensification tubes were glowing in a dim phosphorescent row on a nearby bracket. A man sat in a chair on the platform at the microscope's eyepiece.

I saw all this with a brief glance, then my attention went to a white stone slab under the giant lense. It rested on the platform floor, a two-foot square surface of smooth white marble. A little roped railing a few inches high fenced it. And in its center lay a fragment of golden quartz the size of a walnut!

There was a movement across my line of vision. Two figures advanced. I recognized both of them. And I strained at my bonds; mouthed the gag with futile, frenzied effort. I could no more than writhe; and I couldn't make a sound. I lay, after a moment exhausted, and stared with horror.

The familiar hunched figure of Polter advanced toward the microscope. And with him, his huge hand holding her wrists, was Babs. They were nearly fifty feet from me, but with the light over them I could see them clearly. Babs' slim figure was clad in a long skirted dress — pale blue, now, with the light on it. Her long black hair had fallen disheveled to her shoulders. I couldn't see her face. She did not cry out. Polter was half dragging her as she resisted him; and then abruptly she ceased struggling.

I heard his guttural voice. "That iss better."

They mounted the platform. They were very small and seemed to be far away. I blinked. Horror surged over me. Their figures were dwindling as they stood there. Polter was saying something to the man at the microscope. Other men were nearby, watching. All were normal, save Polter and Babs. A moment passed. Polter was standing by the chair in which the man at the microscope was sitting. And Polter's head barely reached its seat! Babs was clinging to him now. Another moment and they were both tiny figures down by the chair-leg. Then they began walking with swaying steps toward the miniature railing of the white slab. The white reflection from the slab plainly illumined them. Polter's arm was around Babs. I had not realized how small they were until I saw Polter lift the rope of the little four-inch fence, and he and Babs stooped and walked under it. The fragment of quartz lay a foot from them in the center of the white surface. They walked unsteadily toward it. But soon they were running.

My horrified senses whirled. Then abruptly I felt something touch my face! Alan and I were lying in shadow. No one had noticed my writhing movements, and Alan was still in drugged unconsciousness. Something tiny and light and soundless as a butterfly wing brushed my face! I jerked my head aside. On the floor, within six inches of my eyes, I saw the tiny figure of a girl an inch high! She stood, with a warning gesture to her lips — a human girl in a filmy flowing robe. Long, pale golden tresses lay on her white shoulders; her face, small as my little fingernail, colorful as a miniature painted on ivory, was so close to my eyes that I could see her expression — warning me not to move.

There was a faint glow of light on the floor where she stood, but in a moment she moved out of it. Then I felt her brush against the back of my head. My ear was near the ground. A tiny warm hand touched my ear lobe; clung to it. A tiny voice sounded in my ear.

"Please do not move your head. You might kill me!"

There was a pause. I held myself rigid. Then the tiny voice

came again.

"I am Glora, a friend. I have the drug! I will help you!"

CHAPTER III

It seemed that Alan was stirring. I felt the tiny hand leave my ear. I thought that I could hear faint little footfalls as the girl scampered away, fearful that a sudden movement by Alan would crush her. I turned cautiously after a moment and saw Alan's eyes upon me. He too had seen, with a blurred returning consciousness, the dwindling figures of Babs and Polter. I followed his gaze. The while slab with the golden quartz under the microscope seemed empty. The several men in this huge circular dome-room were dispersing to their affairs; three of them sat whispering by what I now saw was a pile of gold ingots stacked crosswise. But the fellow at the microscope held his place, his eyes glued to its aperture as he watched the vanishing figures of Polter and Babs on the rock-fragment.

Alan was trying to convey something to me. He could only gaze and jerk his head. I saw behind his head the figures of the tiny girl on the floor behind him. She wanted evidently to approach his head, but didn't dare. When for an instant he was quiet, she ran forward, but at once scampered back.

From the group by the ingots, one of the men rose and came toward us. Alan held still, watching. And the girl, Glora, seized the opportunity to come nearer. We both heard her tiny voice:

"Do not move! Close your eyes! Make him think you are still unconscious."

Then she was gone, like a mouse hiding in the shadows near us.

Amazement swept Alan's face; he twisted, mouthed at his gag. But he saw my eager nod and took his cue from me.

I closed my eyes and lay stiff, breathing slowly. Footsteps approached. A man bent over Alan and me.

"Are you no conscious yet?" It was the voice of a foreigner, with a queer, indescribable intonation. A foot prodded us. "Wake up!"

Then the footsteps retreated, and when I dared to look, the man was rejoining his fellows. It was a strange looking trio. They were heavy-set men in leather jackets and short, wide knee-length trousers. One wore tight, high boots, and the others a sort of white buckskin, with ankle straps. All were bare-headed — round, bullet heads of close-clipped black hair.

I suddenly had another startling realization. These men were not of normal size as I had assumed! They were eight or ten feet tall at the very least! And they and the pile of ingots, instead of being close to me, were more distant than I had thought.

Alan was trying to signal me. The tiny girl was again at his ear, whispering to him. And then she came to me.

"I have a knife. See?" She backed away. I caught the pin-point gleam of what might have been a knife in her hand. "I will get a little larger. I am too small to cut your ropes. You lie still, even after I have cut them."

I nodded. The movement frightened her so that she leaped backward; but she came again, smiling. The three men were talking earnestly by the ingots. No one else was near us.

Glora's tiny voice was louder, so that we both could hear

it at once.

"When I free you, do not move or they may see that you are loose. I get larger now — a little larger — and return."

She darted away and vanished. Alan and I lay listening to the voices of the three men. Two were talking in a strange tongue. One called to the man at the microscope, and he responded. The third man said suddenly:

"Say, talk English. You know damn well I can't understand that lingo."

"We say, McGuire, the two prisoners soon wake up."

"What we oughta do is kill 'em. Polter's a fool."

"The doctor say, wait for him return. Not long, what you call three, four hours."

"And have the Quebec police up here lookin' for 'em? An' that damn girl he stole off the Terrace. What did he call her, Barbara Kent?"

"These two who are drugged, their bodies can be thrown in a gully down behind St. Anne. That what the doctor plan to do, I think. Then the police find them — days maybe from now — and their smashed airship with them."

Gruesome suggestion!

The man at the microscope called, "They are almost gone I can hardly see them any more." He left the platform and joined the others. And I saw that he was much smaller than they — about my own size possibly.

There seemed six men here altogether. Four now, by the ingots, and two others far across the room where I saw the dark entrance of the corridor-tunnel which led to Polter's castle.

Again I felt a warning hand touch my face, and saw the figure of Glora standing by my head. She was larger now — about a foot tall. She moved past my eyes; stood by my mouth; bent down over my gag. I felt the cautious slide of a tiny knife-blade inserted under the fabric of the gag. She hacked, tugged at it, and in a moment ripped it through.

She stood panting from the effort. My heart was pounding with fear that she would be seen; but the man had turned the central light off when he left the microscope, and it was far darker here now than before.

I moistened my dry mouth. My tongue was thick, but I could talk.

"Thank you, Glora."

"Quiet!"

I felt her hacking at the ropes around my wrists. And then at my ankles. It took her a long time, but at last I was free! I rubbed my arms and legs; felt the returning circulation in them.

And presently Alan was free. "George, what —" he began.

"Wait," I whispered. "Easy! Let her tell us what to do."

We were unarmed. Two, against these six, three of whom were giants.

Glora whispered, "Do not move! I have the drugs. But I can not give them to you when I am still so small. I have not enough. I will hide — there." Her little arm gestured to where, near us, half a dozen boxes were piled. "When I am large as you, I come back. Be ready, quickly to act. I may be seen. I give you then the drug."

"But wait," Alan whispered. "Tell us —"

"The drug to make you large. Large enough to fight these men. I had planned to do that myself, until I saw you held captive. That girl of your world the doctor just now steal, she is friend of yours?"

"Yes! But —" A thousand questions were springing in my mind, but this was no time to ask them. I amended, "Go on! Hurry! Give us the drug when you can."

The little figure moved away from us and disappeared.

Alan and I lay as we had before. But now we could whisper. We tried to anticipate what would happen; tried to plan, but that was futile. The thing was too strange, too astoundingly fantastic.

How long Glora was gone I don't know. I think, not over three or four minutes. She came from her hiding place, crouching this time, and joined us. She was, probably, of normal Earth size — a small, frail-looking girl something over five feet tall. We saw now that she was quite young, still in her teens. We lay staring at her, amazed at her beauty. Her small oval face was pale, with the flush of pink upon her cheeks — a face queerly, transcendingly beautiful. It was wholly human, yet somehow unearthly, as though unmarked by even the heritage of our Earthly strifes.

"Now! I am ready." She was fumbling at her robe. "I will give you each the same."

Her gestures were rapid. She flung a quick glance at the distant men. Alan and I were tense. We could easily be discovered now, but we had to chance it. We were sitting erect. Alan murmured:

"But what do we do? What happens? What —"

On the palm of her hand were two pink-white pellets. "Take these — one for each of you. Quickly!"

Involuntarily we drew back. The thing abruptly was gruesome, frightening. Horribly frightening.

"Quickly," she urged. "The drug is what you call highly radioactive. And volatile. Exposed to the air, it is gone very soon. You are afraid? No, I assure you it is not harmful."

With a muttered curse at his own reluctance, Alan seized the small pellet. I stopped him.

"Wait!"

The men momentarily were engaged in a low-voiced, earnest discussion. I dared to hesitate a moment longer.

"Glora, where will you be?"

"Here. Right here. I will hide."

"We want to go after Mr. Polter," I gestured. "Into the little piece of golden rock. That's where he went with the Earth girl, isn't it?"

"Yes. My world is there — within an atom there in that rock."

"Will you take us?"

"Yes! But later."

Alan whispered vehemently, "Why not now? We could get smaller, now."

But she shook her head. "That is not possible. We would be seen as we climbed the platform and crossed the white slab."

"No," I protested, "not if we get very small, hiding here first."

She was smiling, but urgently fearful of this delay. "Should we get that small, then it would be, from here" — she gestured toward the microscope — "to there, a journey of very many miles. Don't you understand?"

This thing so strange!

Alan was plucking at me. "Ready, George?"

"Yes."

I put the pellet on my tongue. It tasted slightly sweet, but seemed to melt quickly and I swallowed it hastily. My heart, was pounding, but that was apprehension, not the drug. A thrill of heat ran through my veins as though my blood were on fire.

Alan was clinging to me as we sat together. Glora again had vanished. In the background of my whirling consciousness the sudden thought hovered that she had tricked us; done to us something diabolical. But the thought was swept away in the confused flood of impressions upon me.

I turned dizzily. "You all right, Alan?"

"Yes, I — I guess so."

My ears were roaring, the room seemed whirling, but in a moment that passed. I felt a sudden growing sense of lightness. A humming was within me — a soundless tingle. The drug had gone to every tiny microscopic cell in my body. The myriad pores of my skin seemed thrilling with activity. I know now that it was the exuding volatile gas of this disintegrating drug. Like an aura it enveloped me, acted upon my garments.

I learned later much of the principles of this and its companion drug but I had no thought for such things now. The huge dimly illumined room under the dome was swaying. Then abruptly it steadied. The strange sensations within me were lessening, or I forgot them, and I became aware of externals.

The room was shrinking! As I stared, not with horror now, but with amazement and a coming triumph, I saw everywhere a slow, steady, crawling movement. The whole place was dwindling. The platform, the microscope, were nearer than before, and smaller. The pile of ingots, and men near there, were shifting toward me.

"George! My God — this is weird!"

I saw Alan's white face as I turned toward him. He was growing at the same rate as myself evidently, for in all the scene he only was unchanged.

We could feel the movement. The floor under us was shifting, crawling slowly. From all directions it contracted as though it was being squeezed beneath us. In reality our expanding bodies were pushing outward.

The pile of boxes which had been a few feet away, were thrusting themselves at me. I moved incautiously and knocked them over. They seemed small now, perhaps half their former size. Glora was standing behind them. I was sitting and she was standing, but across the litter our faces were level.

"Stand up!" she murmured. "You all right now. I hide!"

I struggled to my feet, drawing Alan up with me. Now! The time for action was upon us! We had already been discovered. The men were shouting, clambering to their feet. Alan and I stood swaying. The dome-room had contracted to half its former size. Near us was a little platform, chair and microscope. Small figures of men were rushing at us.

I shouted, "Alan! Watch yourself!"

We were unarmed. These men might have automatic weapons. But evidently they did not. Only knives were in their hands. The whole place was ringing with shouts. And then a shrill siren alarm from outside started clanging.

The first of the men — a few moments before he had seemed a giant — flung himself upon me. His head was lower than my shoulders. I met him with a blow of my fist in his face. He toppled backward; but from one side another figure came at me. A knife-blade bit into the flesh of my thigh.

The pain seemed to fire my brain. A madness descended upon me. It was the madness of abnormality. I saw Alan with two dwarfed figures clinging to him. But he threw them off, and they turned and ran.

The man at my thigh stabbed again, but I caught his wrist and, as though he were a child, whirled him around me and flung him away. He landed with a crash against the shrunken pile of gold nuggets and lay still.

The place was in a turmoil. Other men were appearing from outside. But they now stood well away from us. Alan backed against me. His laugh rang out, half hysterical with the madness upon him as it was upon me.

"God! George, look at them! So small!"

They were now hardly the height of our knees. This was

now a small circular room, under a lowering concave dome. A shot came from the group of Pygmy figures. I saw the small stab of flame, heard the zing of the bullet.

We rushed, with the full frenzy of madness upon us — enraged giants. What actually happened I cannot recount. I recall scattering the little figures; seizing them; flinging them headlong. A bullet, tiny now, stung the calf of my leg. Little chairs and tables under my feet were crashing. Alan was lunging back and forth; stamping; flinging his tiny adversaries away.

There were twenty or thirty of the figures here now. I feared that they might produce more up-to-date weapons. But my fears were unfounded: soon I saw these figures making their escape.

The room was littered with wreckage. I saw that by some miracle of chance the microscope was still standing, and I had a moment of sanity.

"Alan! Watch out! The microscope — the platform! Don't smash them! And Glora be careful not to hurt her!"

I suddenly became aware that my head and my shoulders had struck the dome roof. Why, this was a tiny room! Alan and I found ourselves backed together, panting in the small confines of a circular cubby with an arching dome close over us. At our feet the platform with the microscope over it hardly reached our boot tops. There was a sudden silence, broken only by our heavy breathing. The tiny forms of humans strewn around us were all motionless. The others had fled.

Then we heard a small voice. "Here! Take this! Quickly! You are too large. Quickly!"

Alan took a step. And sudden panic was on us both. Glora was here at our feet. We did not dare turn; hardly dared to move. To change position might have crushed her now that she had left her hiding place. My leg hit the top of the microscope cylinder. It rocked but did not fall.

Where was Glora? In the gloom we could not see her. We were in a panic.

Alan began, "George, I —"

The contracting inner curve of the dome bumped gently against my head. Our panic and confusion turned into cold fear. The room was closing in to crush us.

I muttered, "Alan! I'm going out!" I braced myself and heaved against the side and top curve of the dome. Its metal ribs and heavy translucent, reinforced glass plates resisted me. There was an instant when Alan and I were desperately frightened. We were trapped, to be crushed in here by our own horrible growth. Then the dome yielded under our smashing blows. The ribs bent; the plates cracked.

We straightened, pushed upward and emerged through the broken dome, with head and shoulders towering into the outside darkness and the wind and snow of the blizzard howling around us.

CHAPTER IV

"Glora — that was horrible!"

We stood, again in normal size, with the wrecked dome-laboratory around us. The dome had a great jagged hole halfway up one of its sides, through which the snow was falling. The broken bodies strewn around were gruesome.

Alan repeated, "Horrible, Glora. The power of this drug is diabolical."

Glora had grown large after us and had given us the companion drug. I need not detail the strange sensations of our dwindling. We were so soon to experience them again!

We had searched, when still large, all of Polter's grounds. Some of his men undoubtedly escaped, made off into the blizzard. How many, we never knew. None of them ever made themselves known again.

We were ready to start into the atom. The fragment of golden quartz still lay under the microscope on the white square of stone slab. We had hurried with our last preparations. The room was chilling. We were all inadequately dressed for such cold.

I left a note scribbled on a square of paper by the microscope. With daylight Polter's wrecked place would be discovered and the police would surely come.

Guard this piece of golden quartz. Take it at once, very care-

fully, to the Royal Canadian Scientific Society. Have it watched day and night. We will return.

I signed it George Randolph. And as I did so, the extra ordinary aspect of these events swept me anew. Here in Polter's weird place I had been living in some strange fantastic realm. But this was the Province of Quebec, in civilized Canada. These were the Quebec authorities I was addressing.

I flung the thoughts away. "Ready, Glora?"

"Yes."

Then doubts assailed me. None of Polter's men had gotten large enough to fight us. Evidently he did not trust them with the drug. We could well believe that, for the thing misused, was diabolical beyond human conception. A single giant, a criminal, a madman, by the power of giant size alone, could menace and destroy beyond belief. The drug lost, or carelessly handled, could get loose. Animals, insects eating it, could roam the Earth, gigantic monsters. Vegetation nourished with the drug, might in a day overrun a big city, burying it with jungle growth!

How terrible a thing, if the realm of smallness were suddenly to emerge, consume this awe inspiring drug! Monsters of the sea, marine organisms, could expand until even the ocean was too small for them. Microbes of disease, feeding upon it —

Alan was prodding me. "We're ready, George."

"Okay, let's go."

This was not the largeness we were facing now, but smallness. I thought of Babs, down there with Polter, beyond the vanishing point in the realm of infinitely small. They had been gone an hour at least. Every moment lost now was adding to Babs' danger.

Glora sat with us on the platform. Strange little creature! She was wholly calm now; methodical with her last directions. There had been no time for her to tell us anything about herself. Alan had asked her why she had come here and how she had gotten the drugs. She waved him away.

"On the way down. Plenty of time then."

"How long will it take us?" Alan demanded.

"Not too long if we are careful with managing the trip. About ten hours."

And now we were ready to start. She told us calmly:

"I will give you each your share of the drugs, but then you take only as I tell you."

She produced from her robe several small vials a few inches long. They were tightly stoppered. The feel of them was cool and sleek; they seemed to be made of some strange, polished metal. Some of them were tinted black while the others glowed opalescent. She gave each of us one vial of each kind.

"The light ones are for diminishing," she said. "We take them very carefully, one small pellet only at first."

Alan was opening one of his, but she checked him.

"Wait! The drug evaporates very quickly. I have more to say. First we sit here together. Then you follow me to the white slab. We climb upon the little rock."

She laid her hands on my arms. Her blue eyes regarded us earnestly. Her manner was naive; childlike. But I could not mistake her intelligence or the force of character stamped on her face for all its dainty, ethereal beauty.

"Alan —" She smiled at him, and tossed back a straying lock of her hair which was annoying her. "You pay attention, Alan. You are very young, reckless. You listen. We must not be separated. You understand that, both of you? We will be always in that little piece of rock. But there will be miles of distance. And to be lost in size —"

What a strange journey upon which we were now starting! Lost in size?

"You understand me? Lost in size. If that happens, we might never find each other. And if we come upon the Doctor Polter and the girl he holds captive — if we can overtake them —"

"We must!" I exclaimed. "And we must get started."

She showed us which pellet to select. They were of several sizes, I found. And as she afterward told us, the larger ones were not only larger but of an intensified strength. We took the smallest. It was barely a thousandth part of the strength of the largest. In unison we placed the pellets on our tongues, and hastily swallowed.

The first sensations were as before. And, familiar now, they caused no more than a fleeting discomfort. But I think I could never get used to the outward strangeness!

The room in a moment was expanding. I could feel the platform floor crawling outward beneath me, so that I had to hitch and change my position as it pulled. We were seated together, Alan and I on each side of Glora. My fingers were on her arm. It did not change size, but it slowly drew away with a space opening between us. Overhead, the dome roof, the great jagged hole there, was receding, lifting, moving upward and away.

Glora pulled us to our feet. "We had better start now. The distance grows very far, so quickly."

We had been sitting within five feet of the stone slab with its four inch high railing around it. A chair was by the microscope eyepiece. As we stood swaying I saw that the chair was huge, and its seat level with my head. The great barrel-cylinder of the microscope slanted sixty feet upward. The dome roof was a distant spread three hundred feet up in the dimness. The dome-room was a vast arena now.

Alan and I must have hesitated, confused by the expanding scene — a slow, steady movement everywhere. Everything was drawing away from us. Even as we stood together, the creeping platform floor was separating us.

A moment passed. Glora was urging us on vehemently:

"Come! You must not stand there!"

We started walking. The railing around the slab was knee-high. The slab itself was a broad, square surface. The fragment of golden quartz lay in its center. It was now a jagged lump nearly a foot in diameter.

The platform seemed to shift as we walked; the railing hardly came closer as we advanced toward it. Then suddenly I realized that it was receding. Thirty feet away? No, now it was more than that — a great, thick rope, waist-high, with a huge spread of white surface behind it.

"Faster!" urged Glora. We ran, and reached the railing. It was higher than our heads. We ran under it, and cut out upon the white slab — a level surface, larger now than the whole dome-room had been.

Glora, like a fawn, ran in advance of us, her robe flying in the wind. She turned to look back.

"Faster! Faster, or it will be too hard a climb!"

Ahead lay a golden mound of rock. It was widening; raising its top steadily higher. Beyond it and over it was a vast dim distance. We reached the rock, breathless, winded. It was a jagged mound like a great fifty-foot butte. We plunged upon it and began climbing.

The ascent was steep; precipitous in places. There were little gullies, which expanded as we climbed up them. It seemed as if we would never reach the top, but at last we were there. I was aware that the drug had ceased its action. The yellow, rocky ground was no longer expanding.

We came to the summit and stood to get back our breath. Alan and I gazed with awe upon the top of a rocky hill. Little buttes and strewn boulders lay everywhere. It was all naked rock, ridged and pitted, and everywhere yellow-tinged.

Overhead was distance. I could not call it a sky. A blur was there — something almost but not quite distinguishable. Then I thought that I could make out a more solid blur which might be the lower lens of the microscope above us. And there were blurred, very distant spots of light, like huge suns masked by a haze, and I knew that they were the hooded lights of the laboratory room.

Before us, over the brink of a five hundred-foot drop, a great glistening plain stretched into the distance. I seemed to see where it ended in a murky blur. And far higher than our hilltop level a horizontal streak marked the rope railing of the slab.

"Well," said Alan. "We're here." He gazed behind us, back across the rocky summit which seemed several hundred feet across to its opposite brink. He was smiling, but the smile faded. "Now what, Glora? Another pellet?"

"No. Not yet. There is a place where we go down. It is marked in my mind."

I had a sudden ominous sense that we three were not alone up here. Glora led us back from the cliff. As we picked our way among the naked crags, it seemed behind each of them an enemy might be lurking.

"Glora, do you know if any of Dr. Polter's men might have the drug? I mean, do they come in and out of here?"

She shook her head. "I think not. He lets no one have the drug. He trusts not anyone. I stole it. I will tell you later. Much I have to tell you before we arrive."

Alan made a sudden, sidewise leap, and dashed around a rock. He came back to us, smiling ruefully.

"Gets on your nerves, all of this. I had the same idea you had, George. Might be someone around here. But I guess not." He took Glora's hand and they walked in advance of me. "We haven't thanked you yet, Glora," he added.

"Not needed. I came for help from your world. I followed the Dr. Polter when he came outward. He has made my world and my people, his slaves. I came for help. And because I have helped you, needs no thanks."

"But we do thank you, Glora." Alan turned his flushed, earnest face back to me. I thought I had never seen him so handsome, with his boyish, rugged features and shock of tousled brown hair. The grimness of adventure was upon him, but in his eyes there was something else. It was not for me to see it. That was for Glora; and I think that even then its presence and its meaning did not escape her.

We reached a little gully near the center of the hilltop. It was some twenty feet deep.

Glora paused. "We descend here."

The gully was an unmistakable landmark — open at one end, forty feet long, with the other end terminating in a blind wall which now loomed above us.

"A pit is here — a hole. I cannot tell just how large it will look when we are in this size."

We found it and stood over it — a foot-wide circular hole extending downward. Alan knelt and shoved his hand and arm into it, but Glora sprang at him.

"Don't do that!"

"Why not? How deep is it?"

She retorted sharply, "The Doctor Polter is ahead of us. How far away in size, who knows? Do you want to crush him, and crush that young girl with him?"

Alan's jaw dropped. "Good Lord!"

We stood with the little pit before us, and another of the pellets ready.

"Now!" said Glora.

Again we took the drug, a somewhat larger pellet this time. The familiar sensations began. Everywhere the rocks were creeping with a slow inexorable movement, the landscape expanding around us. The gully walls drew back and upward. In a moment they were cliff walls and we were in a broad valley.

We had been standing close together. We had not moved, except to shift our feet as the expanding ground drew them apart. I became aware that Alan and Glora were a distance from me. Glora called:

"Come, George! We're going down — quickly now."

We ran to the pit. It had expanded to a great round hole some six feet wide and equally as deep. Glora let herself down, peered anxiously beneath her, and dropped. Alan and I followed. We jammed the pit; but as we stood there, the walls were receding and lifting.

I had remarked Glora's downward glance, and shuddered. Suppose, in some slightly smaller size, Babs had been among these rocks!

The pit widened steadily. The movement was far swifter now. We stood presently in a great circular valley. It seemed fully a mile in diameter, with huge encircling walls like a crater rim towering thousands of feet into the air. We ran along the base of one expanding wall, following Glora.

I noticed now that overhead the turgid murk had turned into the blue of distance. A sky. It was faintly sky-blue, and seemed hazy, almost as though clouds were forming. It had been cold when we started. The exertion had kept us fairly comfortable; But now I realized that it was far warmer. This was different air, more humid, and I thought the smell of moist earth was in it. Rocks and boulders were strewn here on the floor of this giant valley, and I saw occasional pools of water. There had been rain recently!

The realization came with a shock of surprise. This was a new world! A faint, luminous twilight was around us. And then I noticed that the light was not altogether coming from overhead. It seemed inherent to the rocks themselves. They glowed, very faintly luminous, as though phosphorescent.

We were now well embarked upon this strange journey. We seldom spoke. Glora was intent upon guiding us. She was trying to make the best possible speed. I realized that it was a case of judgment, as well as physical haste. We had dropped into that six-foot pit. Had we waited a few moments longer, the depth would have been a hundred feet, two hundred, a thousand! It would have involved hours of arduous descent — if we had lingered until we were a trifle smaller!

We took other pellets. We traveled perhaps an hour more. There were many instances of Glora's skill. We squeezed into a gully and waited until it widened; we leapt over expanding caverns; we slid down a smooth yellowish slide of rocks, and saw it behind and over us, rising to become a great spreading ramp extending upward into the blue of the sky. Now, up there, little sailing white clouds were visible. And down where we stood it was deep twilight, queerly silvery with the dim light from the luminous rocks, as though some hidden moon were shining.

Strange, new world! I suddenly envisaged the full strangeness of it. Around me were spreading miles of barren, naked landscape. I gazed off to where, across the rugged plateau we were traversing, there was a range of hills. Behind and above them were mountains; serrated tiers; higher and more distant. An infinite spread of landscape! And, as we dwindled, still other vast reaches opened before us. I gazed overhead. Was it — compared to my stature now — a thousand miles, perhaps even a million miles up to where we had been two or three hours ago? I thought so.

Then suddenly I caught the other viewpoint. This was all only an inch of golden quartz — if one were large enough to see it that way!

Alan had been trying to memorize the main topographical features of our route. It was not as difficult as it seemed at first. We were always far larger than normal in comparison to our environment, and the main distinguishing characteristics of the landscape were obvious — the blind gully, with the round pit, for instance, or the ramp slide.

We had been traveling some three or four hours when Glora suggested a rest. We were at the edge of a broad canyon. The wall towered several hundred feet above us; but a few moments before, we had jumped down it with a single leap!

The last pellet we had taken had ceased its action. We sat down to rest. It was a wild, mountainous scene around us, deep with luminous gloom. We could barely see across the canyon to its distant cliff wall. The wall beside us had been smooth, but now it was broken and ridged. There were ravines in it, and dark holes resembling cave-mouths. One was near us. Alan gazed at it apprehensively.

"I say, Glora, I don't like sitting here."

I had been telling her all we knew of Polter. She listened quietly, seldom interrupting me. Then she said:

"I understand. I tell you now about Polter as I have seen him."

She talked for five or ten minutes. I listened, amazed, awed by what she said.

But Alan's insistence interrupted her. "Come on, let's get out of here. That tunnel-mouth, or cave, or whatever it is —"

"But we go in there," she protested. "A little tunnel. That is our way to travel. We are not far from my city now."

Perhaps Alan felt what once was called a hunch, a premonition, the presage of evil which I think comes strangely to us more often than we realize. Whatever it was, we had no time to act upon it. The tunnel-mouth which had caused Alan's apprehension was about a hundred feet away. It was a ten-foot, yawning hole in the cliff. Perhaps Alan sensed a movement in there. As I turned to look at it a great, hairy human arm came out of the opening! Then a shoulder! A head!

The giant figure of a man came squeezing through the hole on his hands and knees! He gathered himself, and as he stood erect, I saw that he was growing in size! Already he was twenty feet tall compared to us — a thick-set fellow, dressed in leather garments, his legs and arms heavily matted with black hair. He stood swaying, gazing around him. I stared up at his round bullet head, his villainous face.

He saw us! Stupid amazement struck him, then comprehension.

He let out a roar and came at us!

CHAPTER V

Glora shouted, "Into the tunnel! This way!" She held her wits and darted to one side, with Alan and me after her. We ran through a narrow passage between two fifty-foot boulders which lay close together. Momentarily the giant was out of sight, but we could hear his heavy tread and panting breath. We emerged having passed him. He was taller now. He seemed confused at our sudden scampering activity. He checked his forward rush, and ran around the twin boulders. But we had squeezed into a narrow ravine. He could not follow. He threw a rock. To us it was a boulder. It crashed behind us. To him, we were like scampering insects; he could not tell which way we were about to dart.

Alan panted, "Glora, does this lead out?"

The little ravine seemed to open fifty feet ahead of us. Alan stopped, seized a chunk of rock, flung it up. I saw the giant's face above us. He was kneeling to reach in. The rock hit him on the forehead — a pebble, but it stung him. His face rose away.

Again we emerged. The tunnel-mouth was near us. We reached it and flung ourselves into its ten-foot width just as the giant came lunging up. He was far larger than before. Looking back, I could see only the lower part of his legs blocked against the outer light.

"Glora! Alan, where are you?"

For a moment I did not see them. It was darker in this tunnel of broken rocky walls, and jagged arching roof than outside.

Then I heard Alan's voice: "George! Over here!"

They came running to me. For a moment we stood, undecided. My eyes were becoming accustomed to the gloom. The tunnel was illumined by a dim phosphorescence from the rocks. I saw Alan fumbling for his vials, but Glora stopped him.

"No. We are the right size."

We were about a hundred feet back from the opening. The giant's legs disappeared. But in a moment the round, light hole of the exit was obscured again. His head and shoulders! He was lying prone. His great arms came in. He hitched forward. The width of his expanding shoulders wedged.

I think that he expected to reach us with a single snatch of his tremendous arms. Or perhaps he was confused, or forgot his growth. He did not reach us. His shoulders stuck. Then suddenly he was trying to back out, but could not!

It was only a moment. We stood in the radiant gloom of the tunnel, confused and frightened. The giant's voice roared, reverberating around us. Anger. A note of fear. Finally stark terror. He heaved, but the rocks of the opening held solid. Then there was a crack, a gruesome rattling, splintering — his shoulder bones breaking. His whole gigantic body gave a last convulsive lunge, and he emitted a deafening shrill scream of agony.

I was aware of the tunnel-mouth breaking upward. Falling rocks — an avalanche, a cataclysm around us. Then light overhead.

The giant's crushed body lay motionless. A pile of boulders, rocks and loose metallic earth was strewn upon his head and torso, illumined by the outer light through a jagged rent where the cliff-face had fallen down.

We were unhurt, crouching back from the avalanche. The giant's mangled body was still expanding; shoving at the litter of loose rocks. In a moment it would again be too small for the broken cliff opening.

I found my wits. "Alan, we've got to get out of here. God — don't you see what's happening?"

But Glora restrained us. She realized that the effect of the drug the giant had taken was about at its end. The growth presently stopped. That huge noisome mass of pulp which once had been human shoulders no longer expanded.

I shoved Glora away. "Don't look!" I was shaking; my head was reeling. Alan's face, painted by the phosphorescence, was ghastly.

Glora pulled at us. "This way! The tunnel is not too long. We go."

But the giant had drugs, and perhaps weapons. "Wait!" I urged. "You two wait here. I'll climb over him."

I told them why, and ran. I can only leave to the imagination that brief exploratory climb. The broken body seemed at least a hundred feet long; the mangled shoulders and chest filled the great torn hole in the cliff. I climbed over the litter. Indescribable, horrible scene! A river of warm blood was flowing down the declivity outward. . . .

I came back to Glora and Alan. Under my arm was a huge cylinder vial. It was black, the enlarging drug. I set it down. They stared at me in my bloodstained garments.

"George! You're —"

"His blood, not mine." I tried to smile. "Here's the drug he carried. Evidently Polter was only sending him out because I found just the one drug."

"What'll we do with it?" Alan demanded. "Look at the

size of it!"

"Destroy it," said Glora. "See, that is not difficult." She tugged at the huge stopper, and exposed a few of the pellets — to us as large as apples. "The air will soon spoil it."

We left it in the tunnel. I also had with me a great roll of paper which had been folded in the giant's belt, with the drug cylinder. We unrolled it, and hauled its folds to a spread some ten feet long. It was covered with a scrawled handwriting in pencil, but its giant characters seemed thick blurred strokes of charcoal. We could not read it; we were too close. Alan and Glora held it up against the tunnel wall. From a distance I could make it out. It was a note written in English, signed "Polter," evidently to one of his men.

It read:

The two prisoners, kill them at once. That is better. It will be too dangerous to wait for my return. Put their bodies with their airplane. Crash it a mile from my gate.

Full directions for our death followed. And Polter said he would return by dawn or soon after.

That gave me a start. By dawn! We had been traveling four or five hours. It was already dawn up there now!

"No," Glora explained, "the time in here is different. A different time-rate. I do not know how much difference. My world speeds faster; yours is very slow. It is not the dawn up there quite yet."

Again my mind strove to encompass these things — so strange. A faster time-rate prevailed in here? Then our lives were passing more quickly. We were living, experiencing things, compressed into a shorter interval. It was not apparent: there was nothing to which comparison could be made. I recalled Alan's description of Polter — not thirty years old as he should have been, but nearer fifty. I could understand that, now. A day in here was equal to only a few hours on our gigantic world outside.

We walked the length of the tunnel. I suppose it was a quarter of a mile, to us in this size. I wound through the cliff with a steady downward slope. And suddenly I realized that we had turned downward nearly half the diameter of a circle! We had turned over — or at least it seemed so. But the gravity was the same. I had noticed from the beginning very little change.

The realization of this tunnel brought a mental confusion. I lost all sense of direction. The outer world of Earth was under my feet, instead of overhead. Then we went level. I forgot the confusion: this was normality here. We turned upward a little. Cross tunnels intersected ours at intervals. I saw caverns, open, widened tunnels, as though this mountain were honeycombed.

"Look!" said Glora. "There is the way out. All these passages lead the same way."

There was a glow of light ahead. I recall that I was at that moment fumbling at my belt in two small compartments in which I was carrying the two vials of the drugs which Glora had given me. Alan wore the same sort of belt. We had found them in the wrecked dome-room. I heard a click on the ground at my feet. I was about to stoop to see what I had kicked — only a loose stone, perhaps — but Glora's words distracted me. I did not stoop. If only I had, how different events might have been!

The glow of light ahead of us widened as we approached, and presently we stood at the end of the tunnel. A spread of open distance was outside. We were on a ledge of a steep rocky wall some fifty feet above a wide level landscape. Vegetation! I saw trees — a forest off to the left. A range of naked hills lay behind it. A mile away, in front and to the right, a little town nestled on the shore of shining water. There was starlight on the water! And over it a vast blue-purple sky was studded with stars.

I gazed, with that first sudden shock of emotion, into the infinite depths of interplanetary space! Light years of distance. Gigantic worlds, blazing suns off there shrunken by distance now to little points of light. A universe was here!

But this was an inch of golden quartz!

Above my head were stars which, compared to my bodily size now, were vast worlds ten thousand light-years away! Yet, from the other viewpoint, I had only descended perhaps an eighth, or a quarter of an inch, beneath the broken pitted surface of a little fragment of golden quartz the size of a walnut — into just one of its myriads of golden atoms!

CHAPTER VI

"My world," Glora was saying. "You like it? See the star-light on the lake? I have heard that your world looks like this at night, in summer. Ours is always like this. No day, no night. Just like this — starlight." Her hand went to Alan's shoulder. "You like it? My world?"

"Yes, Glora. It's very beautiful."

There was a sheen on everything, a soft, glowing sheen of phosphorescence from the rocks rising to meet the pale wan starlight. The night air was soft, with a gentle breeze that rip-pled the distant lake into a great spread of gold and silver light.

The city was called Orena. I saw at once that we were about normal size in relation to its houses and people. There were fields beneath our ledge, with farm implements lying in them; no workers, for this was the time for sleep. Ribbons of roads wound over the country, pale streamers in the starlight.

Glora gestured, "The giants are on their island. Everyone sleeps now. You see the island off there?"

Beyond the city, over the low stone roofs of its flat-topped dwellings, the silver spread of lake showed a green-clad is-land some three miles off shore. The distance made its white stone houses seem small. But as I gazed, I realized that they were large compared to their environment, all far larger than those of the little town. The island was perhaps a mile in length. Between it and the mainland a boat was coming toward us. It was a dark blob of hull on the shining water, and above it a queerly shaped circular sail was puffed out, like a balloon parachute, by the wind.

"The giants live there?" said Alan. "You mean Polter's men?"

"And women. Yes."

"Are there many giants?"

"No."

"How many?" I put in. "How large are they? In relation to us now, I mean. And to your normal size?"

"You ask so many questions so fast, George. There are two hundred or more of the giants. And there are more than that many thousands of our people, here. Slaves, because the giants are four times as large. This little city, these fields, these hills of stone and metal, all this was ours to have in peace and happiness until your Polter came."

She gestured. "Everywhere is a great reach of desert and forest. There are insects, but no wild beasts — nothing to harm us. Nature is kind here. The weather is always like this. We were happy, until Polter came."

"And only a few thousand people," Alan said. "No other cities?"

"What lies off in the great distance, we do not know. Our nation is ten times what is here. We have a few other cities, and some of our people live in the forests."

She broke off. "That boat is coming for Polter. He is in the city no doubt of that. The boat will take him and that girl you call Babs, to the giant's island. His castle is there."

I turned to Alan. "They must have arrived only recently. Before we go any further we have to decide what size to be. We can't be gigantic because I'm sure he'd kill Babs if he sees us. We've got to plan!"

If we could get on that boat and go with him to the island — But in what size? Very small? But then, if we were very small it would take us hours to get from here to the boat. Glora pointed out where it would land — just beyond the village where the houses were set in a sparse fringe. It would be there, apparently, in ten or fifteen minutes. Polter probably was there now with Babs, waiting for it.

In our present size we could not get there in time. It was two or three miles at least. But a trifle larger — the size of one of Polter's giants — we would be able to make it. We would be seen, but in the pale starlight, keeping away from the city as much as possible, we might only be mistaken for Polter's people. And when we got closer we would diminish our size, creep into the boat, get near Babs and Polter and then plan what to do.

We climbed down from the ledge and stood at the base of the towering cliff which reared its jagged wall against the stars. A field and a road were near us. The road seemed of normal size. A man was in the field. He was apparently about my height. He presently discarded his work, walked away from us and vanished.

"Hurry, Glora." Alan and I stood beside her while she took pellets from her vials. We wanted our stature now to be four times what it was. Glora gave us pellets of both drugs, one of which was slightly more intense than the other.

"Polter made them this way," she said. "The two taken at once give just the growth to take us from this normal size to the stature of the giants."

Alan and I did not touch our own vials. We had used none of our enlarging drug upon the journey, and the supply she had given us of the other was almost gone.

As I took these pellets which Glora now gave us, standing

there by the side of that road, I recall that I was struck with the realization that never once upon this journey had I conceived myself to be other than normal stature. I am normally about six feet tall. I still felt — there in that golden atom — the same height. This landscape seemed of normal size. There were trees nearby — spreading, fantastic-looking growths with great strings of pods hanging from them. But still — as I looked up to see one arching over me with its blue-brown leaves and an air-vine carrying vivid yellow blossoms — whatever the size of the tree, I could only conceive of myself as a normal man of six-foot stature standing beneath it. The human ego always supreme! Around each man's consciousness of himself the entire universe revolves.

We crouched on the ground when this growth now began; it would not do to be observed changing size. Polter's giants never did that. Years before, he had made them large — his few hundred men and women. They were, Glora said, people both of this realm and from our great world above — dissolute criminal characters who had now set themselves up here as the nucleus of a ruling race.

In a moment now, we were the size of these giants. Twenty to twenty-five feet tall, in relation to the environment. But I did not feel so. As I stood up — still feeling myself in normal stature — I saw around me a shrunken little landscape. The trees, as though in a Japanese garden, were about my own height; the road was a smooth, level path; the little field near us had a toy fence around it. On another road nearby a man was walking. In height he would barely have reached my knees. He saw us rise beside the trees. He darted off in alarm, and disappeared.

I have taken longer to tell all this than the actual time which passed. We could see the boat coming from the island, and it was still a fair distance off shore. We ran along the road, skirting the edge of the little town. None of its houses were taller than ourselves. The windows and doorways were ovals into which we could only have inserted a head or an arm. Most of them were dark. Little people occasionally stared out, saw us run past, and ducked back, thankful that we did not stop to harass them.

"This way," said Glora. She ran like a faun, hardly winded, with Alan and me heavily panting behind her. "There are trees — thick trees — quite near where the boat lands. We can get in them and hide and change our size to smallness. But hurry, for we shall need a great deal of time when we are small!"

The little spread of town and the shining lake remained always to our right. In five minutes we were past most of the houses. A patch of woods, with thick, interlacing treetops about our own height, lay ahead. It extended a few hundred feet over to the lake shore. The sailboat was heading in close. There was a broad starlit roadway at the edge of the lake, and a dock at which the boat was preparing to land.

Would we be in time? I suddenly feared not. To get small now, with distance lengthening between us and the boat, would be disastrous. And where was Polter?

Abruptly we saw him. There had been only little people visible to us: none of our own height. The lake roadway by the dock was brightly starlit. As we approached the intervening patch of woods it seemed that a crowd of little people were near the dock. Polter must have been sitting. But now he rose up. We could not mistake his thick hunched figure, the lump on his shoulders clear in the starlight with the gleaming lake as a background. The crowd of little figures were milling around his knees. In the silence of the night the murmur of their voices floated over to us.

"There he is!" Alan gasped. We all three checked our running; we were at the edge of the patch of woods. "By God, there he is! Let's get larger and rush him! He's only a few hundred feet away!"

But Babs? Where was Babs?

"Alan, get down!" I crouched, pulling Alan and Glora with me. "Don't let him see us! We can't rush him Alan, 'til we find Babs. He'd see us coming and kill her."

Of all the strange events that had been flung at us, I think this sudden crisis now most confused Alan and me. . . . To get larger, or smaller? Which? Yet something had to be done at once.

Glora said, "We can get through the woods best in this size. We won't be seen and will be closer to the landing."

We crouched so that the treetops were always well over us. The patch of woods was dark. A soil of black loam was under us, a thick soft underbrush reached our knees, and lacy, flexible leaves and branches were about shoulder height. We pushed them aside, forcing our way softly forward. It was not far. The little murmuring voices of the crowd grew louder.

Presently we were crouching at the other edge of the woods. I softly shoved the tree branches aside until we could all three get a clear view of the strange scene now directly before us.

And I saw a toy dock, at which a twenty-foot, bargelike open sailboat was landing; a narrow starlit roadway, crowded with a milling throng of people all no more than a foot and a half in height. The crowd milled almost to where we were crouching, unseen in the shrubbery.

Across the road by the dock, Polter stood with the crowd down around his knees. In height he seemed the old familiar Polter. Bareheaded, with his shaggy black hair shot with white. He was dressed in Earth fashion: narrow black evening trousers and a white shirt and collar with flowing black tie. I saw at once what Alan had noticed — the change in him. An abnormality of age. I would have called him now forty, or older. Beyond even that there was an abnormality. A man old before his time; or younger than he should have been for the years he had lived. An indescribable mingling of something of the two worlds, perhaps. It marked him with a look at once unnatural and sinister.

These were instant impressions. Glora was plucking at me. "On the white chest of his shirt, something is there."

Polter was coatless, with snowy white shirt and cuffs to his thick wrists. He was no more than fifty feet from us. On his shirt bosom something golden in color was hanging like a large bauble, an ornament, an insignia. It was strapped tightly there with a band about his chest, a cord, like a necklace chain, up to his thick hunched neck, and other chains down to his belt.

I stared at it. An ornament, like a cube held flat against his shirt front — a little golden cube, ornate with tiny bars.

I heard Alan murmuring, "A cage! Why George, it's —"

And then, simultaneously, realization struck me. It was a golden cage strapped there. And I seemed to see that there was something in it. A tiny figure? Babs!

"I think he has her there," Glora murmured. "You see the little box with bars? The girl, Babs, is a prisoner in there." She spoke swiftly, vehemently. "He will take the boat to the island."

She gripped us. "You think it really best to go? I do what you say. I had the wish to get to my father with these drugs."

"No!" exclaimed Alan. "We must keep close to Polter!"

We were ready with our pellets. But a sudden activity in the road made us pause. The crowd of little people were hostile to Polter. A sullen hostility. They milled about him as he stood there, gazing down at them sardonically.

And abruptly he shouted at them in English. "You speak my language, some of you. Then listen!"

The crowd fell silent.

"Listen. This iss your future Queen. Can you see her? She iss small now. But she has the magic power. Soon she will be large, like me."

The crowd was shouting again. It surged forward, but it lacked a leader, and those in advance shoved backward in fear.

Polter spoke again. "This girl from my world, you will like her. She iss kind and very beautiful. When she iss large, you will see how beautiful."

A small stone suddenly came up from the throng of little people and struck Polter on the shoulder. Then another. The crowd, emboldened, made a rush: surged against his legs.

He shouted, "You do that? Why, how dare you? I show you what giants do when you make dem angry!"

From down by his knees he plucked the small figure of a man. The crowd scattered with shouts of terror. Polter had the struggling eighteen-inch figure by the wrist. He whirled it around his head like a ninepin and flung it over the canopy of the dock far out into the shimmering lake!

CHAPTER VII

The trees around us expanded to towering forest giants. The underbrush rose up over our heads. We had taken a taste of the diminishing drug. Glora showed us how to touch it to our tongue several times, to adjust our size as we became smaller. It took us no more than a minute to diminish. We could hear the roar of the crowd, and Polter's voice shouting. We ran forward through the great forest. It was a fair distance out to the starlit road. We saw it as a wide shining esplanade. The people now were giants twice our height! Polter, himself towering with a seeming fifty-foot stature, was standing by the gigantic canopy of the dock. He had dispersed the crowd. There was an open space on the esplanade — a run for us of about a hundred feet.

"We've got to chance it," I murmured. "Make a run for it — now."

We darted across. In the confusion, with all eyes centered on Polter, we escaped discovery. It was dim under the dock canopy. Polter had backed from the road and was walking to the barge. It lay like the length of an ocean liner, its sail looming an enormous spread above it. The gunwale was level with the dock. A dozen or more fifty-foot men were greeting Polter. They were amidships.

I realize now that in those moments as we scurried

aboard like wharf rats, we took wild chances. We made for the stern which momentarily was unoccupied. To Polter and his men we were eight or nine inches tall. We dropped over the gunwale, slid down the thirty or forty-foot incline of the interior and landed on the bottom of the boat.

There were many places where we could safely hide. A litter of gigantic rope-strands was around us. We could see the bottom of a crossbench looming over head, and the great curving sides of the vessel with the gunwales outlined against the starlight.

The boat left the dock in a moment; the sail bellied out, enormous over us. Ten feet forward from us the towering figure of a man sat on a bench with the steering mechanism before him. Further on, the other men were dispersed, with one or two in the distant bow. Polter reclined on a cushioned couch amidships. Looking along the dark widely level bottom of the boat there were only the feet and legs of men visible.

Alan whispered, "Let's get closer."

We were insects soundlessly scuttling unnoticed in the dimness. It was noisy down here — the clank of the steering mechanism; the swish and surge of the water against the hull; the voices of the men.

We passed the boots of the seated helmsmen, and found another hiding place nearer Polter. We could see his giant length plainly. None of the other men were near him. He was reclining on an elbow, stretched at ease on a cushion. And at the moment, he was fumbling with the chains that fastened the little golden cage to his chest. The cage was double its former size to us now. A shaft of pale light came down, reflected from the great sail surface overhead. It struck the bars of the cage. We could see a small figure in there.

Then we heard Polter's voice. "I will let you out, Babs. You come out, sit on my hand and talk with me. That will be nice? We haf a little time."

He unfastened the cage and put it on the cushion beside him. He was still propped up on one elbow.

"I let you out, now. Be careful, Babs."

My heart was almost smothering me. "Alan! We've got to get still closer! Try something! Get large, shall we?"

Alan whispered tensely, "I don't know! I don't know what to do."

"We can get closer," Glora whispered. "But never larger — not here. They would discover us too soon."

We crept forward. We reached the edge of the cushion. Its top surface was a trifle lower than our heads — a billowing, wrinkled mass of fabric. But I saw that the folds of it were rough enough to afford a footing. I thought that I could climb it. We stood erect. There was a deep shadow along here, but it was brighter on the cushion top. We could see over its edge; an undulating spread of surface with the giant length of Polter stretched over it. The cage was near us. Polter's great fingers fumbled with it; a door in the lattice bars flipped open.

"Careful, my Babs!" His voice was a throaty, rumbling roar above us. "Careful! I do not want you to be hurt."

From the little doorway came the figure of Babs! The starlight glowed on her blue dress; her black hair was tumbling over her shoulders; her face was pale but she was unharmed.

I think that I had never loved her so much as at that moment. Nor ever seen her so beautiful as in miniature, standing at the door of her golden cage, bravely facing the monstrous misshapen figure of her captor.

We heard her small voice.

"What do you want me to do?"

"Stand quiet. Now I put my hand for you."

His monstrous hand bristled with a thatch of heavy black

hair. He slid it carefully along the cushion. Babs was barely the length of one of its finger joints. She climbed upon its palm.

"That iss right, Babs. Now I bring you — hold tight to my finger. Here, I crook the little one. Fling your arms around it."

With a swoop his hand took her aloft and away. Then we saw her, twenty feet or so in the air, still on his hand as he held it near his face.

"Now we haf a little talk, Babs. When we get to the island, I put you back in your cage."

I had a sudden flash of realization. There was something I could do. I know now my judgment was bad. I recall it struck me that Alan would want to do it also. And, perhaps, even Glora. But that wouldn't work. My chances, however desperate, were better alone. Glora and Alan — in our present size — could doubtless disembark safely. Glora knew the layout of the island. And she could follow Polter.

Alan and Glora were standing beside me peering over that billowing cushion spread toward the distant giant palm with Babs standing upon it. I gripped Alan's shoulder.

"See here, Alan," I whispered vehemently: "What ever happens, we must follow Polter. Glora knows the way. Some opportunity will come to get large without being discovered. Then we'll rush Polter!"

Alan's white face turned to me. "Yes, that's what we're planning. But George, here on this boat —"

"Of course not. Can't do it here. Tell Glora, to be sure to follow Polter. Whatever happens, you'll think of nothing else: you won't will you?"

"George, what —"

"We've got to make some opportunity." I was trembling inside, fearful that Alan would be suspicious of me. Yet I had to make sure that he and Glora would stay as close to Polter as possible.

"All right," Alan agreed. "Listen to them."

Polter was talking to Babs. But I didn't hear the words I moved a trifle away. Rash decision! I hardly decided anything. There was only the vision of Babs before me and my love for her. My desperate need of doing something; getting to her, seeing her, being with her. I wanted her near my own size again as though the blessed normality of that would rationalize and lessen her danger. If only I had been less rash! If only back there in that tunnel I had stopped to see what it was my foot kicked against!

I slid away. Alan and Glora did not notice it; they were whispering together and gazing over the cushion at Babs. In the shadow of the cushion I moved some ten feet. On the undulating top of the cushion the little golden cage stood with its lattice door open. It was a few feet from my face.

I fumbled at my belt for the diminishing vial. I found one pellet left. Well, that would be enough. I was hurried. Alan might discover me. Polter might put Babs back in the cage and close its door. We might be near the island already, and the confusion, the activity of disembarking would defeat me. A thousand things might happen.

I touched the pellet to my tongue. In a few seconds the drug action had come and passed. The cushion top loomed well over my head. The side was a ridged, indescribably unnatural vista of cliff wall. The fabric was coarse with hairy strands, dented into little ravines and crevices. I climbed and I came panting to the pillow surface. The golden cage was six or eight feet away and was now two feet high.

Again I touched the drug to my tongue; held it an instant. The cage drew away; grew to a normal six-foot height; then larger, until in a moment it stopped. I stood peering at it, trying to gauge its size in relation to me. I wanted so intensely now to appear normal in Babs' eyes. The cage seemed about ten feet high. A little less, possibly. I barely tasted the pellet, and replaced it carefully in the vial. I could only hope its efficacy would be preserved.

I had to chance that I wouldn't be seen while crossing this billowy expanse. I ran. The rope strands of the fabric now had spaces between their curving surfaces. The cage was a shining golden house, set on this wide rolling area. Far in the distance there was a blur — Polter's reclining body.

I reached the cage. It was a room about ten feet square and equally as high. Walled solid, top and bottom, and on three sides. The front was a lattice of bars, with a narrow six-foot doorway, standing open now.

I dashed in. The interior was not wholly bare. There was a metal-wrought couch fastened to the wall, with a railing around it and handles. It suggested a ship's bunk. There was a railing at convenient height all around the wall.

I sought a hiding place. I saw just one — under the couch. It was secluded enough. There was a grillelike lattice extending down from the seat to the floor. I squeezed under one end, and lay wedged behind the grille.

How much time passed I don't know. My thoughts were racing. Babs would be coming.

I heard the distant approaching rumble of Polter's voice. Through the grille I could see across the floor of the ten foot cage to the front lattice bars. Outside, there appeared a huge, pink-white, mottled blob — Polter's hand, a ridged and pitted surface with great, bristling black stalks of hair.

The figure of Babs came through the cage doorway. Blessed normality! The same slim little Babs who always stood, since we were both matured, with her head about level with my shoulders.

The latticed door swung shut with a reverberating metallic clank. Babs stood tense, clinging to the wall railing. I heard the blurred rumble of Polter's voice.

"Hold tightly, my little Babs!"

The room lurched; went upward and sidewise with a wild dizzying swoop. Babs clung to the rail and I was wedged prone under the couch. Then the movement stopped; there was a jolting, rocking, and outside I heard the clank of metal. Polter was fastening the chains of the cage to his chest.

A white glow now came through the bars. It was starlight reflecting from Polter's shirt bosom. An abyss of distance was outside. I could see nothing but the white glow.

Momentarily there was very little movement in the room. Only the rhythmic sway of Polter's breathing and an occasional jolt as he shifted his position. The floor was tilted at a sharp angle. Babs came toward the couch, pulling herself along the wall railing.

I called softly, "Babs!"

She stopped. I called again, "Babs! Don't cry out! It's George! Here — stand still!"

She gave a little cry. "George — where are you? I don't —"

I slid out from my concealment and stood up, holding to the railing.

Blessed normality of size! She cried again, "George! You! How did you get here?"

She edged along the railing, a step or two down the tilting floor, then released her hold and flung herself into my waiting arms.

"I think we are landing. Hold on to the railing, George. When the room moves it goes with a rush."

Babs laughed softly. It must have seemed to her, after being alone in here, that now our plight was far less desperate. She had told me how she was captured. A man accosted her on the Terrace, saying he wanted to speak to her about Alan. Then a weapon threatened her. Amid all those people she was held up in old-fashioned style, hurried to a taxicar and whirled away.

She was saying now, "When Polter moves, it is dizzying. You'll see."

"I have already, Babs. Heavens, what a swoop!"

The room was more level now. We carefully drew ourselves to the front lattice. Polter was standing, and we had the white sheen from his shirt front. A sheer drop was outside the bars, but looking down I could see the outlines of his body with the huge spread of the boat's cockpit underneath us.

A confusion of rumbling voices sounded. Blurred giant shapes were outside. The room jolted and swayed as the boat landed and Polter disembarked.

Babs stood clinging to me. We, at least, were normal in this metal barred room, Babs and I. But outside was the abnormality of largeness. I think that in relation to us, the men were of over two hundred-foot stature, and the hunched Polter a trifle less. It seemed as he walked that we were lurching at least a hundred and fifty feet above ground.

"You had better hide," Babs urged. "He might stop and speak to someone. If anyone looked in here you would be seen; no chance then, even to get across the room."

It was true. But for a few moments I lingered. I could distinguish vegetation on their flat roof-tops, as though flower gardens were laid there.

We passed a house with its hundred-foot oval windows all aglow with light. Music floated out — a distant blare of sounds, and the ribald laughter of giant voices. I had seen no women among these giants of the island. But now a huge face was at one of the ovals. A dissolute, painted woman of Earth, staring out at Polter as he passed. It was like the enormous close-up image on a large motion picture screen. She shouted ribald jest as he went by.

"George, please go back. Suppose she had seen you?"

We were ascending a hill. A distance ahead a great oblong building loomed like a giant's palace, which indeed it was. We headed for it, passed through a vast arching doorway into the greater dimness of an echoing interior. I scurried back across the lurching room and again wedged myself under the couch. Babs stood at the lattice ten feet away. We dared to talk in low tones; the rumbling voices and footsteps outside would make our tiny voices inaudible to Polter.

I was tense with my plans. I had told them to Babs. With the one remaining partially used pellet of the diminishing drug we could make ourselves small enough to walk out through the bars. Then my black vial of the enlarging drug, as yet unused, would take us up, out to our own world. We could not use the drugs now. But the chance might come when Polter would set the cage on the ground, or somewhere so that we might climb down from it, with a chance to hide and get large before we were discovered. I would fight our way upward; all I needed was a fair start in size.

But I lay now with doubts assailing me. This was the first moment I had had for calm thoughts, though in truth they were far from calm! Were Alan and Glora following us now? I could only hope so. Once out of this, Babs and I would have to rejoin them. But how? Panic swept me. I shouldn't have left them. Or at least I should have told them what I was trying to do, and given Alan a chance to plan.

The panic grew, the premonition of disaster. From my belt I took the opalescent vial with its one partially used pellet. I dumped the pellet out. It was spoiling! The exposure to the air and the moisture of my tongue, had ruined it! I realized the catastrophe, as I held its crumbling, deliquescing fragments on my palm it melted into vapor and was gone!

We couldn't make ourselves smaller! Now we'd have to wait until Polter opened the cage. But once outside, the enlarging drug would give us our chance to fight our way upward. My trembling fingers sought the black vial in my belt. It wasn't there! My mind flung back: in that tunnel, something had dropped and I had kicked it! Accursed chance! My accursed, heedless stupidity!

I had lost the black vial! We were helpless! Caged! Marooned here in a size microscopic!

CHAPTER VIII

I lay concealed and Babs stood at the lattice of our cage room. I was aware that Polter had entered some vast apartment of this giant palace. The light outside was brighter; I heard voices — Polter's and another man's. I could see the distant monster shape of one. He was at first so far away that all his outline was visible. A seated man in a huge white room. I thought there were great shelves with enormous bottles. The spread of table tops passed under our cage as Polter walked by them. They held a litter of apparatus, and there was the smell of chemicals in the air. This seemed to be a laboratory.

The man stood up to greet Polter. I had a glimpse of his head and shoulders. He wore a white linen coat, open, soft collar and black tie. He seemed an old man, queerly old, with snow-white hair.

I had an instant of whirling impressions. Something was familiar about his face. It was wrinkled and seamed with lines of age and care. There were gentle blue eyes.

Then all I could see was the vast spread of his white shirt and coat, a black splotch of his tie outside our bars as Polter faced him.

Babs gave a low cry. "Why — why — dear God —"

And then I knew! And Polter's words were not needed,

though I heard their rumble.

"I am back again, Kent. Are you still rebellious? You haf still determined to compound no more of our drugs? You would rather I killed you? Then see what I haf here. This little cage, someone —"

It was Dr. Kent whom he addressed. He must have been here all these years!

Babs turned her white face toward me. "George, it's father! He's alive!"

"Quiet, Babs! Don't let him know I'm here. Remember!"

The old man recognized her. "Babs!" It was an agonized cry. The blur of him was gone as he sank down into his chair.

Polter continued standing, I could envisage his sardonic grin.

From over us came Polter's rumble. "She iss glad to see you, Kent. I haf her here, safe. You always knew I would nefer be satisfied until I had my little Babs? Well, now I haf her. Can you hear me?"

A sudden desperate calmness fell on Babs. She called evenly. "Yes, I hear you. Father, don't anger him. Do what he says. Dr. Polter, will you let me be with my father? After all these years, let me be with him, just for a little while. In his size — normal."

"Hah! My Babs iss scheming."

"No, I want to talk to him, after all these years when I thought he was dead."

"Scheming? You think, my little Babs, that he has the drugs? I am not so much a fool. He makes them. He can do that. And that last secret reaction, only he can perform. He iss stubborn. Never would he tell me that one reaction. But he makes no drugs complete, only when I am here."

"No, Dr. Polter! I want only to be with him."

The old man's broken voice floated up to us. "You won't

harm her, Polter?"

"No. Fear nothing. But you no longer rebel?"

"I'll do what you tell me." The tones carried hopeless resignation, years of being beaten down, rebelling — but now this last blow vanquished him. Then he spoke again, with a sudden strange fire.

"Even for the life of my daughter, I will not make your drugs, Polter, if you mean to harm our Earth."

The golden cage room swooped as Polter sat down. "Hah! Now we bargain. What do you care what I do to your world? You never will see it again. I can lie to you. My plans —"

"I *do* care."

"Well, I will tell you, Kent. I am good-natured now. Why should I not be with my dear little Babs? I tell you, I am done with the Earth world. It iss much nicer here. My friends, they haf a good time always. We like this little atom realm. I am going out once more. I must hide the little piece of golden quartz so no harm will come to it."

Polter was evidently in a high good humor. His voice fell to an intimate tone of comradeship; but still I could not mistake the irony in it.

"You listen to me, Kent. There was a time, years ago, when we were good friends. You liked your young assistant, the hunchback Polter. Iss it not so? Then why should we quarrel now? I am gifing up the Earth world. I wanted of it only the little Babs. . . . You look at me so strange! You do not speak."

"There is nothing to say," retorted Dr. Kent wearily.

"Then you listen. I haf much gold above in Quebec. You know that. So very simple to take it out of our atom, grow large with it to what we call up there the size of a hundred feet. I haf a place, a room, secluded from prying eyes under a dome roof. I become very tall, holding a piece of gold. It is large when I am a hundred feet tall. So I haf collected much gold. They think I own a mine. I haf a smelter and my gold quartz I make into ingots, refined to the standard purity. So simple, and I am a rich man.

"But gold does not bring happiness, my friend Kent." He chuckled ironically at his use of the platitude. "There iss more in life than the ownership of gold. You ask my plans. I haf Babs, now. I am gifing up the Earth world. The mysterious man they know as Frank Rascor will vanish. I will hide our little fragment of quartz. No one up there will even try to find it. Then I come down here, with Babs, and we will haf so nice a little government and rule this world. No more of the drugs then will be needed, Kent. When you die, let the secret die with you."

Again Polter's voice became ingratiating, even more so than before. "We will be friends, Kent. Our little Babs will lof me; why should she not? You will tell her — advise her — and we will all three be very happy."

Dr. Kent said abruptly, "Then leave her with me now. That was her request, a moment ago. If you expect to treat her kindly, then why not —"

"I do! I do! But not now. I cannot spare her now. I am very busy, but I must take her with me."

Babs had been silent, clinging to the bars of our cage. She called; "Why? I ask you to put this cage down."

"Not now, little bird."

"Let me be with my father."

It struck a pang through me. Babs was scheming but not the way Polter thought. She wanted the cage put on the floor, herself out, and a chance for me to escape. I had not yet told her of my miserable stupidity in losing the vial.

Polter was repeating, "No, little bird. Presently; not now. I will take you with me on my last trip out. I want to talk with you in normal size when I haf time."

Our room swooped as he stood up. "You think over what I haf said, Kent. You get ready now to make the fresh drugs I will need to bring down all my men from the outer world. They will all be glad to come, or, if not — well, we can easily kill those who refuse. You make the drugs. I need plenty. Will you?"

"Yes."

"That iss good. I come back soon and gif you the catalyst for that last reaction. Will you be ready?"

"Yes."

The blur outside our bars swung with a dizzying whirl as Polter turned and left the room, locking its door after him with a reverberating clank.

*****

Left alone in his laboratory, Dr. Kent began his preparations for making a fresh supply of the drugs. This room, with two smaller ones adjoining, was at once his workshop and his prison. He stood at his shelves, selecting the basic chemicals. He could not complete the final compounds. The catalyst which was necessary for the final reaction would be brought to him by Polter.

How long he worked there with his thoughts in a whirl at seeing Babs, he did not know. His movements were automatic; he had done all this so many times before. His mind was confused, and he was trembling from head to foot — an old, queerly, unnaturally old man now — unnerved. His fingers could hardly hold the test tubes.

His thoughts were flying. Babs was here, come down from the world above. It was disaster — the thing he had feared all these years.

He suddenly heard a voice.

"Father!"

And again: "Father!" A tiny voice, down by his shoe tops.

Two small figures were there on the floor beside him. They were both panting, winded by running. They were enlarging.

It was Alan and Glora, who had followed Polter from the boat, then diminished again and had come running through the tiny crack under the metal door of the laboratory.

They grew to a foot in size, down by Dr. Kent's legs. He was too unnerved to stand; he sat in a chair while Alan swiftly told him what had happened. Babs was in the golden cage. Dr. Kent knew that; but none of them knew what had happened to me.

"We must make you small, Father. We have the drugs, here with us."

"Yes! How much have you? Show me. Oh, my boy, that you are here — and Babs —"

"Don't you worry. We'll get away from him."

Glora and Alan had almost reached Dr. Kent's size before their excited fingers could get out the vials. They took some of the diminishing drug to check their growth. Alan handed his father a black vial.

"Yes, lad —"

"No! Wait, that's the wrong drug. This other —"

Dr. Kent had opened the vial. His trembling hand spilled some of the pellets, but none of them noticed it.

"Father, this one." Alan held an opalescent vial. "Take this one."

Glora said abruptly, "Listen! Is that someone coming?"

They thought they heard approaching footsteps. A moment passed but no one came into the room.

"Hurry," urged Glora. "That was nothing. We're waiting too long."

"My boy — Alan, after all these years —"

As they were about to take the diminishing drug a very queer sound came from across the room. A scuttling, scratching, and the drone of wings.

"God, Father — look!"

Over by the wall, a giant fly was running across the floor. The fly had eaten some of the sweetish powder.

The enlarging drug was loose!

A few drops of water lay mingled with the drug on the floor. And from the water nameless hideous things were rising!

CHAPTER IX

To Alan the first moments that followed the escape of the drug were the most horrible of his life. The discovery struck old Dr. Kent, Glora and Alan into a numb, blank confusion. They stood transfixed, staring with cold terror at the fly which was scurrying along the floor close to the wall. It was already as large as Alan's hand. It ran into the corner, hit the wall in its confused alarm, and turned back. Its wings were droning with an audible hum. It reared itself on its hairy legs, lifted and sailed across the room.

As though drawn by a magnet, Alan turned to watch it. It landed on the wall. Alan was aware of Dr. Kent rushing with trembling steps to a shelf where bottles stood. Glora was stricken into immobility, the blood draining from her face.

The fly flew again. It passed directly over Alan. Its body, with a membrane sac of eggs, was now as large as his head; its widespread transparent wings were beating with a reverberating drone.

Alan flung a bottle which was on the table beside him. It missed the fly, crashed against the ceiling, came down with splintering glass and spilling liquid. Fumes spread chokingly over the room.

The fly landed again on the floor. Larger now! Expanding with a horribly rapid growth. Glora flung something — a little wooden rack with a few empty test tubes in it. The rack struck the monstrous fly, but did not hurt it. The fly stood with hairy legs braced under its bulging body. Its multiple eyes were staring at the humans. And with its size must have come a sense of power, for it seemed to Alan that the monstrous insect was abnormally alert as it stood measuring its adversaries, gathering itself to attack them.

Only a few seconds had passed. Confused thoughts swept Alan. This fly with its growth would soon fill this room. Burst it; burst upward through a wrecked palace; soar out, and by the power of its size alone devastate this world.

He heard himself shouting, "Father, get back! It's too large! I've *got* to kill it!"

Could he wrestle with it and hope to win? Alan edged around the center table. He was bathed in cold sweat. This thing was horrifying! The fly was already half the length of his own body. In a moment it might be twice that! He was aware of Glora pulling at him, and his father rushing past him with a bottle of liquid, shouting:

"Alan! Run! You and the girl, get out of here! Into the other room —"

Then Alan saw the things on the floor! His foot crushed one with a slippery squash! Nameless, hideous, noisome things grown monstrous, risen from their lurking invisibility in the drops of water! Sodden, gray-black and green-slimed monsters of the deep; palpitating masses of pulp! One lay rocking, already as large as a football with streamers of ooze hanging from it, and squirting a black inky fluid. Others were rods of red jelly-pulp, already as large as lead pencils, quivering, twitching. Disease germs, these ghastly things, enlarging from the invisibility of a drop of water!

The fly landed with a thud on the center table. The fumes of the shattered bottle of chemicals were choking Alan. He flung himself toward the monster fly, but Glora held him.

"No! Escape to the other room!"

Dr. Kent was stamping the things upon the floor; pouring acids upon them. Some eluded him. The air in the room was unbreathable. . . .

Alan and Glora reached the bedroom. The laboratory was a hideous chaos. They were aware of its outer door opening, disclosing the figure of Polter who, undoubtedly, had been attracted by the noise. He shouted a startled oath. Alan heard it above the beating wings of the monstrous fly. Things lurched at the opened door; Polter banged it upon them and rushed away, shouting the alarm through the palace.

Dr. Kent was stammering, "Not the enlarging drug, Glora, child, the other! Hurry!"

Alan helped Glora with the opalescent vial. Things were lurching toward this room, from the laboratory. Alan, with averted face, choked by the incoming fumes, slammed the door upon the gruesome turmoil.

They took the diminishing drug. The bedroom expanded. The hideous sounds from the laboratory, and the whole palace now ringing with a wild alarm, soon faded into blessed remoteness of distance. . . .

"I think this is the way, Alan. Off there — a doorway from my bedroom. Polter always kept it locked, but it leads into a corridor. We must get out of here. A crack under the door — is that it, off there?" Dr. Kent pointed into the gloomy blur of distance. "We're horribly small — it's so far to run — and I've lost my sense of direction."

The drug had ceased its action. The wooden floor of the room had expanded to a spread of cellular surface, ridged with broken, tubelike tunnels; pits and jagged cave-mouths. A knothole yawned like a crater a hundred feet away.

"We are too small," Glora protested hurriedly. "The door

is where you say, Dr. Kent, but miles away."

With the other drug, the room contracted. The floor surface shrank and smoothed a little. The door was distinguishable — a square panel several hundred feet in width and towering into the upper haze. The black line of the crack was visible along its bottom.

They ran to it. The top of the crack was ten feet above their heads. They ran under, across the wide intervening darkness toward a glow of light. Then they came from under the door into a corridor — and shrank against a cliff wall as with a rush of wind and pounding tread the blurred shapes of a man's huge feet and legs rushed past. The upper air was filled with rumbling shouts.

"We must chance it!" exclaimed Dr. Kent. "It's too far in this size. We must get larger — and if they see us, we'll fight our way out!"

In the turmoil of the doomed palace no one noticed them. They cast aside all restraint. It was too dangerous to wait. The excessive dose they took of the drug made the corridor shrink with dizzying speed. They rushed along its length. Alan hurled a little man aside who was in their path. They were already larger than Polter's people.

They squeezed out of a shrinking doorway. The dwindling island was a turmoil. Little figures were pouring from the palace. At the edge of the water. Alan, Glora and Dr. Kent stood for an instant looking behind them. The palace was rocking. Its roof heaved upward and then smashed and fell aside with the clatter of tumbling masonry. The monstrous fly, its hideous face mashed and oozing, reared itself up and, with broken torn wings, tried to soar away. But it could not. It slipped back. The drone and buzz of its fright sounded over the chaos of noise. Other things came lurching and twisting upward, slithering out. . . .

The expanding body of the fly was pushing the palace walls outward. In a moment it collapsed and the fly emerged.

To Alan and his companions the scene was all shrinking into a miniature chaos of horror at their shoe tops. A diminuendo of screams mingled down there. Overhead were the stars, shining peacefully remote. Nearby lay a rapidly narrowing channel of shining water. A tiny city was across it. Lights were moving. The panic had spread from the island to Orena. Beyond the tiny city, was a range of mountains, a cliff, gleaming in the starlight, and tunnel-mouths.

Suddenly against the stars off there, Alan saw the enlarging figure of Polter, his hunched shape unmistakable. He was facing the other way. He lunged and scrambled into a yawning black hole in the mountains. Polter was escaping! None of these people except himself had the drugs. He was escaping with the golden cage, out of this doomed atomic world to the Earth above.

Glora murmured, "There is our way out. Your way. And that is Polter going. I do not think he saw us. So much is growing gigantic here."

Dr. Kent muttered, "We will wait a moment — wade across — or leap over, and follow him out. Babs is with him — dear God I hope so! This is a doomed realm!"

Alan held Glora close. And suddenly he was laughing — a madness, half hysterical. "Why, this, all this — why look, Glora, it's funny! This little world all excited, an ant-hill, outraged! Look! There's our giant sailboat!"

Down near their feet the inch-long sailboat stood at its dock. Tiny human figures were rushing for it; others, floundering in the water, were trying to climb upon it. Dr. Kent had stepped a foot or two from the shore, and tiny, lashing white rollers rocked the boat, almost engulfing it.

Alan's laugh rang out. "God! It's funny, isn't it? All those little creatures so excited!"

"Steady, lad!" Dr. Kent touched him. "Don't let yourself laugh! A moment now, then we'll wade across. Polter won't have much start on us. We mustn't get too close to him in size, but try and attack him unawares. We've got to get Babs away from him."

The narrowing passage rose hardly to their knees. They stepped ashore, well to one side of the toy city. Their growth had almost stopped. But suddenly Alan realized that Glora was diminishing! She had taken the other drug.

"Glora! What are you doing?"

"I must go back, Alan. This is my world, doomed perhaps, but I cannot forsake it now. I must give the enlarging drug to my father. And others who can rise and fight these monsters."

"Glora!"

Dr. Kent said hurriedly, "She's right, Alan. There is a chance they can save their city. For her to leave them would be dastardly."

She cried, "You go on up, Alan. You have enough of the drugs. I am going back!"

"No," he protested. "You can't! If you do, I'm coming with you!"

She clung to him. He felt her body diminishing within his encircling arms. His love for her swept him — this girl who had cajoled Polter, or tricked him and stolen several of the vials from him, heavens knows how, and followed him up to the other world. This girl whom Alan had come to love, was leaving him, perhaps forever.

As he stood there, with the miniature landscape at his feet in the wan starlight — the panic-stricken tiny city, the island with its monsters rising to overwhelm this tiny world — it seemed to Alan that if he let her go it was the end for him of all life's promised happiness.

"Alan, lad, come." His father was pulling him along. So horrible a choice! Alan thought that I was back on that island. But Babs, a prisoner in the golden cage, was with Polter, plunging upward in size. And his father was beside him, pleading.

"Alan — come — I can't get out alone, or save Babs. And Polter, with the power of this drug, can conquer and enslave our Earth as he has enslaved Orena — just one little city of one tiny golden atom! Believe me, lad, your duty lies above."

Glora's head was now down at Alan's waist. He stooped and kissed her white forehead; his fingers, just for an instant, smoothed her glossy hair.

"Good-bye, Glora."

She plunged away, and her tread as she dwindled mashed the forest behind the city. Alan and his father ran for the cliff. They were too large to squeeze into the little hole. But in a moment they made themselves smaller. They climbed as they dwindled; checked the drug action and rushed into the tunnel-mouth.

Alan stopped just for an instant to gaze out over the starlit scene. It was almost the same viewpoint from which he had his first sight of Glora's world only an hour or two before. The distant island beyond the city showed plainly with the shining water around it. The vegetation there was growing! And there were dark, horribly formless blobs lurching outward and rising with monstrous bulk against the background of the stars!

"Alan! Come, lad!"

With a prayer for Glora trembling on his lips, Alan plunged into the dim phosphorescent gloom of the tunnel.

CHAPTER X

To Babs and me the ride in the golden cage strapped to Polter's chest as he made his escape outward into largeness was an experience awesome and frightening almost beyond description. We heard the alarm in the palace on the island. Polter rushed to Dr. Kent's laboratory door, looked in, and in a moment banged it shut. Babs and I saw very little. We knew only that something terrible had happened; we could see only a blur with formless things in the void beneath our bars; and there were the choking fumes of chemicals surging at us.

Polter rushed through the castle corridor. We heard rumbling distant shouts.

"The drug is loose! The drug is loose! Monsters! Death for everyone!"

The room swayed with horrible dizzying lurches as Polter ran. We clung to the lattice bars, our legs and arms entwined. There were moments when Polter leaped, or suddenly stooped, and our reeling senses all but faded.

"Babs! Don't let go! Don't lose consciousness!"

If she should be limp, here in this lurching room, her body to be flung back and forth across its confines — that would be death in a moment. I didn't think I could hold her, but I managed to get an arm about her waist.

"Babs, are you all right?"

"I'm — all right, George. I can stand it. We're — he is enlarging."

"Yes."

I saw water far beneath us, lashed into a turmoil of foam with Polter's wading steps. There was a brief swaying vista of a toy city; starlight overhead; a lurching swaying miniature of landscape as Polter ran for the towering cliffs. Then he climbed and scrambled into the tunnel-mouth. Had he turned at that instant doubtless he would have seen the rising distant figures of Glora, Alan and Dr. Kent. But evidently he didn't see them. Nor did we.

Polter spoke only very occasionally to Babs. "Hold tightly!" It was a rumbling voice from above us. He made no move to touch the cage, except that a few times the great blur of his hand came up to adjust its angle.

The lurching and jolting was less violent in the tunnel. Polter's frenzy to escape was subsiding into calmness. He traversed the tunnel with a methodical stride. We were aware of him climbing over the noisome litter of the dead giant's body which blocked the tunnel's further end. We heard his astonished exclamations. But evidently he did not suspect what had happened, thinking only that the stupid messenger had miscalculated his growth and had been crushed.

We emerged into a less dim area. Polter did not stop at the fallen giant. Nothing mattered now to him, quite evidently, save his own exit with Babs from this atomic realm. His movements seemed calm, yet hurried.

We realized now how different an outward journey was from the trip coming in. This was all only an inch of golden quartz! The stages upward were frequently only a matter of growth in size; the distances in this vast desert realm of golden rock always were shrinking. Polter many times stood almost motionless until the closing, dwindling walls made him scramble upward into the greater space above.

It may have been an hour, or less. Babs and I, from our smaller viewpoint, with the landscape so frequently blurred by distance and Polter's movements, seldom recognized where we were. But I realized going out was far easier in every way than coming in. Easier to determine the route, since usually the diminishing caverns and gullies made the upward step obvious. . . . We knew when Polter scrambled up the incline ramp.

It seemed impossible for us to plan anything. Would Polter make the entire trip without a stop? It seemed so. We had no drugs, and our cage was barred beyond possibility of our getting out. But even if we had had the drugs, or had our door been open, there was no escape. An abyss of distance was always yawning beyond our lattice — the sheer precipice of Polter's body from his chest to the ground.

"Babs, we must make him stop. It he sits down to rest you might get him to take you out. I must reach his drugs."

"Yes. I'll try it, George."

Polter was momentarily standing motionless as though gazing around him, judging what to do next. His size seemed stationary. Beyond our bars we could see the distant circular walls as though this were some giant crater-pit in which Polter was standing. Then I thought I recognized it — the round, nearly vertical pit into which Alan had plunged his hand and arm. Above us then was a gully, blind at one end. And above that, the outer surface, the summit of the fragment of golden quartz.

"Babs, I know where we are! If he takes you out, keep his attention. I'll try and get one of his black vials. Make him hold you near the ground. If I see you there, in position where you can jump, I'll startle him. Babs it's desperately dangerous but I can't think of anything else. Jump. Get away from him. I'll keep his attention on me. Then I'll join you if I can — with the drug."

Polter was moving. We had no time to say more.

"I'll try it, George." For just an instant she clung to me with her soft arms about my neck. Our love was sweeping us in this desperate moment, and it seemed that above us was a remote Earth world holding the promise of all our dreams. Or were we cross-starred, doomed like the realm of the atom? Was this swift embrace now marking the end of everything for us?

Babs called, "Dr. Polter?"

We could feel his movements stopping.

"Yes? You are all right, Babs?"

She laughed — a ripple of silvery laughter — but there was tragic fear in her eyes as she gazed at me. "Yes, Dr. Polter, but breathless. Almost dead, but not quite. What happened? I want to come out and talk to you."

"Not now, little bird."

"But I want to." To me it was a miracle that she could call so lightly and hold that note of lugubrious laughter in her voice. "I'm hungry. Didn't you think of that? And frightened. Take me out."

He was sitting down! "You remind me that I am tired, Babs. And hungry, also. I haf a little food. You shall come out for just a short time."

"Thank you. Take me carefully."

Our tilted cage was near the ground as he seated himself. But it was still too far for me to jump.

I murmured, "Babs it's not close enough to the ground."

"Wait, George, I'll fix that. You hide! If he looks in he'll see you."

I scrambled back to my hiding place. Polter's huge fingers were fumbling at our bars. The little door sprang open.

"Come, Babs."

He held the cupped bowl of his hand to the doorway. "Come out."

"No!" she called. "It is too far down!"

"Come. That iss foolish."

"No! I'm afraid. Put the cage on the ground."

"Babs!" His finger and thumb came reaching in to seize her, but she avoided them.

"Dr. Polter! Don't! You'll crush me!"

"Then come out on my hand."

He seemed annoyed. I had scrambled back to the doorway; I knew he couldn't see me so long as the cage remained strapped to his shirt front.

I whispered, "I can make it, Babs!"

Polter was apparently on one elbow now, half turned to one side. From our cage, the sloping gleaming white surface of his stiff glossy shirt bosom went down a steep incline. His belt was down there, and the outward bulging curve of his lap — a spreading surface where I could land like a scuttling insect, unobserved, if only Babs could hold his attention.

I whispered vehemently, "Try it! Go out! Leave me — keep talking to him!"

She called instantly, "All right, then. Bring your hand! Closer! Carefully! It seems so high up here!"

She swung herself into his palm, and flung her arms about the great pillar of his crooked finger. The bowl of his hand moved slowly away. I heard her faint voice, and his overhead rumble.

I chanced it! I didn't know his exact position or which way he was looking.

Again I heard Bab's voice. "Careful, Dr. Polter. Don't let me fall!"

"Yes, little bird."

I let myself down from the tilted doorway, hung by my hand and dropped. I struck the ramp-like yielding surface of his shirt bosom. I slid, tumbling, scrambling, and landed softly in the huge folds of his trouser fabric. I was unhurt. The width of his belt, high as my body, was near me. I shrank against it. I found I could cling to its upper edge.

My hold came just in time. He shifted and sat up. I was lifted with a swoop of movement. When it steadied I saw above me the top of his knee. His left leg was crooked, the foot drawn close to him. Babs was perched up there on the knee summit. His right leg was outstretched. I was at the right side of his belt. I could dart off along that curving expanse of his leg and leap to the ground. If he would hold this position! One of the pouches of his belt was near me. The vial in it was black. The enlarging drug! I moved toward it.

But Babs was too high to jump from that summit of his crooked knee! I think she saw me at his belt. I heard her voice.

"I cannot eat up here. It is too high. Oh, please be careful how you move! I am so dizzy, so frightened! You move with such great jerks!"

He had what seemed a huge surface of bread and meat. He was breaking off crumbs to put before her. I reached the pouch of his belt. The vial was as long as my body. I tugged to try and lift it out.

All the giant contours of Polter's body shifted as he cautiously moved. I clung. I saw that Babs was being held gently between his thumb and forefinger. He lowered her to the ground, and she stood beside the bread and the meat he had placed there.

And she had the courage to laugh! "Why this — this is an enormous sandwich! You will have to break it."

He was leaning over her, half turned on his side. The vial came free. I shoved it; but I could not control its weight. I pushed desperately. It slid over the round brink of his right hip, and fell behind him. I heard the tinkling thud of it down on the rocks.

There was no alarm. I could not chance leaping from his hip. I scurried along the convex top of his outstretched leg, and beyond his knee I jumped.

I landed safely. I could see the black vial back across the broken rock surface, with the bulge of Polter's hip above it. I ran back and reached the vial, tugged at its huge stopper. The cork began to yield under my panting, desperate efforts. In a moment I would have a pellet of the enlarging drug; make away with it and startle Polter so that Babs might dart off and escape.

The huge stopper of the vial was larger than my head. It came suddenly out. I flung it away, plunged in my hand, and seized an enormous round pellet.

Then abruptly the alarm came, and I had not caused it! Polter ripped out a startled, rumbling curse and sat upright. Under the curve of his leg I saw Babs had been momentarily neglected. She was running.

Across the boulder-strewn plain, two tiny men had appeared. Polter had seen them.

They were the enlarging figures of Dr. Kent and Alan!

CHAPTER XI

The astounded Polter was taken wholly by surprise. He had no idea that anyone was following him. He thought he was alone with tiny Babs in this rock-strewn metal desert. What he saw as he scrambled to his feet were four insect-size humans, two of them at a distance, and two within reach of him, and all of them scampering in different directions. The ground was littered with crags and boulders; it was ridged and pitted, pock-marked, with tiny crater-holes and caves. The four scuttling figures almost instantly had disappeared from his sight.

I did not see where Babs went. I turned from the black vial of Polter's enlarging drug, and with the huge pellet under my arm I ran leaping over the rough ground and flung myself into a gully. I lay prone, flattened against a rock. In the murky distance of a pseudo-sky overhead, the monstrous head and shoulders of Polter were visible. I could see down to just below his waist. The empty cage with its door flapping open hung against his shirt-front. He had stooped to try and re-cover Babs. And instinctively his hands went to his belt to seize his enlarging drug.

They were fumbling there now. He hauled out an opalescent vial of the diminishing element. But his black vial was gone. His annoyance turned into fear as he searched for it in the other compartments of his belt. I had thought that he had more than one black vial, but now it seemed not. His huge face was swept with the panic of terror. He glanced wildly around him.

Through the open end of my gully I saw in the distance, miles away, the enlarging figure of Alan rising up. Then it ducked in back of a distant rising peak. Polter undoubtedly saw it. He was fumbling with his opalescent vial. In his confused panic he made the mistake of taking the diminishing drug and instantly seemed to regret it. His curse rumbled above me. His glance went down to the rocks at his feet, and there he saw his black vial lying with its stopper out. His body already was beginning to dwindle. He stooped, seized the vial, and took the enlarging drug. The shock of it mode him stagger; momentarily he disappeared from my line of vision but I could hear his panting breath and the unsteady pound of his footsteps.

I still held that huge round ball of the drug. I seized a loose stone and frantically knocked off a chunk-heaven knows how much. I shoved it into my mouth, chewed and hastily swallowed it. And with the lurching, swaying, shrinking gully closing in upon me, I ran to get out of its distant end.

I was heading toward where Alan and his father were hiding. I came from the gully into the open, just as I the walls closed behind me. The whole scene was a dizzying, blurred sway of contracting movement. I saw that I was in a circular valley now some five miles in diameter, with its jagged enclosing walls rising sheerly perpendicular out of sight in the haze overhead.

Polter had staggered backward. I saw him a mile or so away. His back at that instant was turned to me. He was now no more than three or four times my own height. He scrambled against the valley cliff wall as though trying to find a foothold to climb up it. He went a little way, but fell back.

Near me, Alan and old Dr. Kent suddenly appeared. I was larger than they. Alan gasped with surprise.

"You, George! You got Babs —"

"Yes — Babs is around somewhere! Stay down here! Don't lose her in size! Stay small! Search and —"

"But, George —"

"I'll tackle Polter. I've taken — God, I don't know how much I've taken of the drug!"

They were shrinking down by my boot tops. Alan shouted suddenly, "There's Babs! Thank God, she's all right."

She was so small that I couldn't see her, or even hear her, though she must have been calling to them. Alan again screamed up at me with his little voice:

"She's here, George! You — go on and get Polter! I can't overtake you — haven't enough of the drug!" His tiny voice was fading away. "Go and get him, George! This time — get him —"

I swung with a staggering step around to face the open valley. It had by now shrunk to nearly half a mile in width. Its smooth walls rose some two or three thousand feet to an upper circular horizon with murky distance overhead. Polter stood across from me. He had tried to climb out but could not. He saw me and came lurching. We were a quarter of a mile from each other. I ran forward through a shifting scene of shrinking rock walls and crawling, contracting ground. Quarter of a mile? It seemed hardly more than a score of running strides before Polter loomed close ahead of me. He was still nearly twice my size. I stooped, seized a loose boulder, and flung it. I missed his face, but, as his hand went up carrying a bare knife, by fortunate chance, the stone struck his wrist. The knife dropped to the rocks. He stooped to recover it, but I was upon him. As I felt his huge arms go about me, half lifting me, my foot struck the knife. But in an instant it was swept down into smallness beneath us as we expanded above it.

Both of us now were unarmed in this combat of size. I was an immature youth in Polter's first grip upon me. I heard his panting words, grimly triumphant:

"This — George Randolph, I haf been — waiting for so many years! The hunchback — takes his revenge — now —"

He lifted me. His great arms were unbelievably powerful, but I could feel them dwindling. I was enlarging faster. Just a few moments — if I could last a few moments. . . . My feet were off the ground, my chest pressed close against the little cage between us. He had a hand shoving back my head; his fingers sought my throat. I wound my legs around him, and then he tried to throw me down and fall upon me. But he had twisted and my back was against the cliff. The rocks were shoving at us, insistently pushing with almost a living movement. Polter staggered with me. His grip on my throat tightened, shutting off my breath. My senses whirled. His grim sardonic face over me became blurred. I tore futilely at my throat to break his choking grip. All the world was a roaring chaos to my fading senses. Then in the blur I saw horror sweep his expression. His fingers involuntarily loosened. I got a breath of blessed air, gasping, and my sight cleared.

Walls were closing around us! We were in a pit barely ten feet wide, with the top a few feet above Polter's head. The nearer wall shoved us again. Our bodies almost filled the shrinking pit! Polter lurched and cast me off. I half fell, striking my shoulder against the opposite wall, and I saw Polter leap at the dwindling brink and scramble out.

I was nearly wedged. As I rose, the top of the pit only reached my waist. Polter had fallen on the upper ground, and was on hands and knees. Instead of standing up, he lurched at me trying to shove me back. But I was out; I clutched at him. We were almost of a size now. We rolled on the ground, locked together; rolled to the brink of the pit and over it, as it shrank to a little round hole unnoticed beneath our threshing bodies!

*****

At the side of the circular valley Alan and Dr. Kent crouched with the smaller figure of Babs between them. They saw Polter and me as two swaying gigantic forms locked in a death struggle, towering against the sky. Tremendous expanded bodies! They saw us come to grips; saw the great hunched Polter bend me backward, choking me.

Our bodies lurched. Our huge legs with a single step brought us to the center of the valley. It was a shrinking valley to Alan, Babs and Dr. Kent, for they too, were enlarging. But the fighting giant figures were growing faster. In only a moment their shoulders were up there in the sky, pressing against the narrowing cliff walls.

Alan gasped, "But George will be crushed! Look at him!"

Horror swept them as they crouched, watching. The enormous pillars of Polter's legs towered straight up from near at hand. Alan was aware of himself screaming:

"George, get out! You're too large! Too large for in here!"

As though his microscopic voice could reach me — my head a hundred feet above him. But he screamed it again. This was all in a few horrible moments, though it seemed to the three watchers an eternity. Alan was helpless to aid me; they had taken all of the enlarging drug they had.

Then they saw Polter cast me off. I lurched and struck, with my shoulders wedged against the cliff directly over where they crouched. The overhead sky was darkened as Polter scrambled upward.

Alan was still screaming futilely.

Babs huddled with white horrified face, staring. Then I went out after Polter. My disappearing legs were great dark blurs in the sky. Alan saw the valley now contracted to a thousand feet of width, with its cliffs equally as high. Then everything was smaller. . . . The sky overhead went dark again from cliff to cliff as a segment of rolling bodies momentarily spanned the opening.

Presently Alan realized that the valley had narrowed to a pit. He stood up. "Hurry! Now we can go after them. Up there!"

The opening above was empty. Polter and I were fighting some distance away. . . .

Dr. Kent was soon large enough to scramble out of the pit. Alan handed the little Babs up to him and followed. Alan saw that they were now in a long gully, blind at one end with a five hundred foot perpendicular cliff. Against the wall, the Titanic form of Polter stood at bay. And I was confronting him. The summit of the cliff was lower than our waists. Triumph swept Alan; he saw that I was the larger! As Polter bored into me my backward step crossed the full width of the gully. Alan shouted:

"Down! Babs — Father!"

They had barely time to flatten themselves in a narrow crevice between upstanding rocks before my foot crashed down. For an instant the sole of my foot formed a flat black ceiling as it spanned the rocks. Then it lifted and was gone with a blurred swoop. They saw the white blur of my hand come down and snatch a tremendous boulder, raising it with a great sweep of movement into the sky. They saw me crash it against Polter; but it only struck his shoulder. He roared with anger. The whole sky was roaring and rumbling with our shouts and our panting breathing, and the ground was clattering, pounding with our giant tread. Huge loose boulders were tumbled in an avalanche everywhere.

Again it seemed to Alan that our lurching, heedlessly surging bodies must be crushed within these contracting walls. Only our locked, intertwined legs were visible; our bodies were lost in the sky. Then it seemed to Alan that I had heaved Polter upward. And followed him. We disappeared. There was a distant overhead rumble, and the murky sky, with vague patches of far-distant illumination in it, became empty of movement. . . .

The walls presently were again closing upon Alan and his companions. They ran out of the open end of the shrinking little gully and came to a new upward vista. . . .

*****

I found myself a full head and shoulders taller than Polter. And he was tiring, panting heavily. His face was cut and bleeding from the blows of my fist. The rock I heaved struck his shoulder. He roared, head down, and bored into me. He was heavier than I. His weight flung me back. My foot slid on the loose stones of the gully floor. I did not know that Babs, Alan and their father were huddled under those stones!

My back struck the opposite wall. Polter's upflung knee caught me in the stomach, all but knocking the breath out of me. He was desperate, oblivious to the closing walls. And as he flung his arms with a grip about my neck, hanging, trying to bear down, I saw in his blazing dark eyes what seemed the light of suicide. I think that then, with a sudden frenzied madness he realized that he was beaten, and tried to pull us to the ground and let the walls crush us.

I summoned all my remaining strength and heaved us forward. I broke his hold. His body was jammed back against a lowering wall. Its top seemed almost at our knees. I shoved frantically. He fell backward and I jumped after him.

We were on a great rocky plateau. But it was shrinking,

crawling into itself. Spots of light were in the murk overhead: there seemed a distant circular horizon of emptiness around us.

Polter was lying in a heap. But it was trickery, for as I incautiously bent over him his hand crashed a rock against my head. I reeled, with all the world turning black, but didn't fall. There was a terrible instant when my senses were going, but I fought to hold them. Blood from a wound on my forehead was streaming in my eyes. I was staggering. Then I realized that I was grimly tossing my head, shaking the blood away; and little by little my sight came back.

Polter was on his feet, rushing me. His fist came with an upward swing at my chin, but I ducked.

And suddenly, fighting up there in the open, my mind envisioned how gigantic we were! This was a great upland plateau, rounded with miles of distance and shadowy dimly radiant abyss beyond its circular horizon. And I was a thousand feet or more tall! A Titan, looming here in the sky!

My fist quite unexpectedly caught Polter's jaw. His simultaneous swing went wild, as I leapt backward from it. He staggered, and his arms dropped to his sides. I was crouched forward, guarded, watching him while I gasped for breath. There was the briefest of instant when an expression of vague surprise swept his face. But I had not knocked him out.

It was death overtaking him. His heart was yielding, overtaxed from the strain; and I think that there, at the last, he realized it. The blood drained suddenly from his face and lips, leaving them livid. I saw fear, then a wild horror in his eyes. He stood swaying. Then his knees gave way and he toppled. He fell from his height in the air where I stood gazing at him — fell forward on his face, his Titanic length spread all across the top of this rocky landscape!

For a moment I did not move. My head was reeling, my

ears roaring. Blood streamed into my eyes. I wiped it away with a torn sleeve and stood panting, gazing at the glowing distance around me.

I was a Titan, standing there. The body of Polter was shrinking at my feet. The circular abyss of emptiness came nearer as this rocky eminence contracted.

Suddenly my attention went to the sky overhead. Vague distant lights were there. Then a broad flat blur seemed spread over me. Light everywhere was growing. Beyond the nearby brink of the abyss was a white reflected radiance from beneath. Abruptly I realized there was a level, flat white plain running far off there in the distance.

Overhead a radiance contracted into a spot of light. A shape in the sky moved! I heard a faraway rumble — a human voice!

The body of Polter lay at my feet. It was hardly the length of my forearm. I stood, a Titan.

And then, with a shock of realization, I saw how tiny I was! This was the broken top of that fragment of golden quartz the size of a walnut! I was standing there, under the lens of the giant microscope in Polter's dome-room laboratory, with half a dozen astounded Quebec police officials peering down at me!

CHAPTER XII

I need not detail the aftermath of our emergence from the atom. Dr. Kent and Babs followed me out within a few moments. But Alan was not with them! He had seen Polter fall. His father and Babs were safe. The sacrifice he had made in leaving Glora was no longer needed.

Down there on the rocky plateau, Dr. Kent suddenly realized that Alan was dwindling.

"Father, I have to! Don't you understand? Glora's world is menaced. I can't leave her like this. My duty to you and Babs is ended. I did my best. You two are safe now."

"Alan! You can't go!"

He was already down at Dr. Kent's waist, Babs' size. He held up his hand. "Dad, don't try to stop me. Good-bye." His rugged youthful face was flushed, his voice choked. "You — you've been a mighty good father to me. Always."

Babs flung her arms about him. "Alan. Don't!"

"But I must." He smiled whimsically as he kissed her. "You wouldn't want to leave George, would you? Never see him again? I'm not asking you to do that, am I?"

"But, Alan —"

"You've been a great little pal, Babs. But I have to go."

"Alan! You talk as though you were never coming back!"

"Do I? But of course I'm coming back!" He cast her off.

"Babs, listen. Father's upset. That's natural. You tell him not to worry. I'll be careful, and do what I can to save that little city. I must find Glora and —"

Babs was suddenly trembling with eagerness for him. "Yes! Of course you must, Alan!"

"I'll find her and bring her out here! I'll do it! Don't you worry." He was dwindling fast. Dr. Kent had collapsed to a rock, staring down with horror-stricken eyes. Alan called up to Babs:

"Listen! Have George watch the chunk of gold quartz. Have it guarded and watched day and night. Handle it carefully, Babs!"

"Yes! Yes! How long will you be gone, Alan?"

"How do I know? But I'll come back — don't worry. Maybe in only a day or two of your time."

"Right! Good-bye, Alan!"

"Good-bye," his tiny voice echoed up.

Babs could see his miniature face smiling up at her. She smiled back and waved her arm as he vanished into the pebbles at her feet.

*****

It has broken Dr. Kent. A month now has passed. He seldom mentions Alan to Babs and me. But when he does, he tries to smile and say that Alan soon will return. He has been very ill this last week, though he is better now. He did not tell us that he was working to compound another supply of the drugs, but we knew it very well.

And his emotion, the strain of it, made him break. He was in bed a week. We are living in New York, quite near the Museum of the American Society for Scientific Research. In a room of the biological department there, the precious fragment of golden quartz lies guarded. A microscope is over it, and there is never a moment of the day or night without an alert, keen-eyed watcher peering down.

But nothing has appeared. Neither friend or foe — nothing. I cannot say so to Babs, but often I fear that Dr. Kent will suddenly die, and the secret of his drugs die with him. I hinted that I would make a trip into the atom if he would let me, but it excited him so greatly I had to laugh it off with the assurance that of course Alan would soon return safely to us. Dr. Kent is an old man now, unnaturally old, with, it seems, the full weight of eighty years pressing upon him. He cannot stand this emotion. I think he is despairingly summoning strength to work upon his drugs, fearful that at any moment, he will not be equal to it. Yet more fearful to disclose the secret and unloose such a diabolic power.

There are nights when with Dr. Kent asleep, Babs and I slip away and go to the Museum. We dismiss the guard for a time, and in that private room we sit by the microscope to watch. The fragment of golden quartz lies on its clean white slab with a brilliant light upon it.

Mysterious little golden rock! What secrets are there, down beyond the vanishing point in the realm of the infinitely small? Our human longings go to Alan and Glora.

But sometimes we are swept by the greater viewpoint. Awed by the mysteries of nature, we realize how very small and unimportant we are in the vast scheme of things. We envisage the infinite reaches of astronomical space overhead. Realms of largeness unfathomable. And at our feet, everywhere, a myriad entrances into the infinitely small. With ourselves in between — with our fatuous human consciousness that we are of some importance to it all!

Truly there are more things in Heaven and Earth than are dreamed of in our philosophy!

THE END

www.ingramcontent.com/pod-product-compliance
Lightning Source LLC
Chambersburg PA
CBHW030537180626
46810CB00005B/1903